About the Author

This is the author's second published novel. The author lives in Sussex.

Russell Appleby

J. M. Drummond

Russell Appleby

Vanguard Press

VANGUARD PAPERBACK

© Copyright 2024
J. M. Drummond

The right of J. M. Drummond to be identified as author of this work has been asserted by him in accordance with the Copyright, Designs and Patents Act 1988.

All Rights Reserved

No reproduction, copy or transmission of this publication may be made without written permission.
No paragraph of this publication may be reproduced, copied or transmitted save with the written permission of the publisher, or in accordance with the provisions of the Copyright Act 1956 (as amended).

Any person who commits any unauthorised act in relation to this publication may be liable to criminal prosecution and civil claims for damages.

A CIP catalogue record for this title is available from the British Library.

ISBN 978 1 80016 906 7

This is a work of fiction. Names, characters, businesses, places, events and incidents are either the product of the author's imagination or used in a fictitious manner. Any resemblance to actual persons, living or dead, or actual events is purely coincidental.

*Vanguard Press is an imprint of
Pegasus Elliot Mackenzie Publishers Ltd.*
www.pegasuspublishers.com

First Published in 2024

**Vanguard Press
Sheraton House Castle Park
Cambridge England**

Printed & Bound in Great Britain

Chapter 1

A skylark sings as it takes flight from a field full of growing barley under an early sun one fine spring morning. The little bird flits through the sky over the fields towards a small village nestled in a valley. It flies high over a set of old houses that surround a green in the centre of the village, then drops downwards towards a figure lying flat out on the dew-covered grass. The figure, also covered in dew, lying flat out on the village green, is Geoffrey Wade.

He lies face down in a thin layer of mud, snoring loudly. His lips quiver when he releases a never-ending series of loud snores from his heavily unshaven face, blowing bubbles into the watery mud beneath him. He looks to have been lying in the same position, next to the pond in the middle of the village, for some time judging by the early morning dampness over the back of his old, long, brown overcoat and on the back of his unkempt hair.

Suddenly, there is a jerking movement from the seemingly lifeless body inside the coat that scares the interested and hovering skylark swiftly away and back up high into the sky.

Geoffrey Wade moves his face out of the mud and awakens slightly, bringing the loud snores to an end. He wipes his mouth free of dried sputum, then opens his eyes to let in a stream of bright sunshine that soon makes him quickly close them again.

A burst of crowing from a cockerel in a field close by brings Geoff a pained expression that doesn't leave his face for as long as the cock continues the noise. Can the cockerel see this drunken man in the long overcoat from where it crows? Perhaps the cockerel can but whether it can or not, it keeps crowing loudly and very annoyingly as the sun begins to rise above them both.

As much as Geoff tries, he can no longer rest with the cockerel's insistent racket ringing in his ears. The agonised expression that has been fixed on Geoff's face now increases, when he opens his eyes and looks into the bright sunlight above him. Geoff squints to keep out some of the light but because he is now fully awake, he is forced to wrestle with the drunken stupor that now fills his every pore.

Geoff opens his dry mouth. He needs to drink water. There's a pond ahead of him that he now remembers from the night before. Perhaps he took a drink from this very same pond last night but for now he cannot remember doing so.

He struggles to his feet, then staggers towards the pond feeling very poorly indeed. He bends down towards the water but his body feels very stiff. He can bend down no further, so he just walks into the pond until the water unsteadies him and he falls face first into it with a splash.

Geoff drinks the pond water thirstily until he feels refreshed. He then pulls himself to his feet and stands in the middle of the shallow pond to look into the sun above him so as to try and get his bearings. The cockerel continues to crow. Geoff cannot remember another time when he's heard a cockerel crow so loudly and for so long. He instinctively feels that it is crowing purposely to mock him and had it been closer, he feels sure that he would have silenced it by now.

A galloping of horses hooves soon echoes too loudly around him through the early morning mist. His bloodshot eyes focus on a moving blur that develops more clearly as it approaches him. The blur turns into an early-morning sport galloping his horse along the small country lane that wraps itself around the village green, towards the pond where he now stands.

The early-morning sport leans over his horse to inspect the scene in the middle of the pond.

"I say there, are you all right?" says the early-morning sport in a clear and loud manner towards the wet, bedraggled and unwell-looking man knee-deep in the centre of the pond.

Geoff does not reply because of his unwell feeling and a real desire not to speak to this annoying and spritely sounding young man on the back of a horse. Instead Geoff replies in the only manner that seems appropriate to him: he collapses once more into the pond.

The early-morning sport jumps down from his horse then dashes across the village green towards the pond. He wades into the water, turns Geoff over so that he is no longer face-down in the water, then slowly drags him towards the side of the pond. Geoff rouses when he feels himself being pulled towards dry land so he blows out a stream of water from his mouth to somehow signify to his rescuer that he still breathes.

The morning sport lays Geoff down by the side of the pond as a gaggle of ducks waddling on the far side begin to quack loudly in his direction, almost as if they are laughing at him – which, perhaps, they are.

"Damn you! Damn you all! Get away with you, whoever you are!" shouts Geoff, into the face of the shocked horse rider.

"I say, that's no way to speak to your rescuer," replies the morning sport.

"I couldn't give a damn what you say, who you are, or what you are doing here! Damn you away from here!" shouts Geoff, struggling to get up onto the slippery, dewy surface of the grass.

The insulted horse rider jumps back atop his horse then gallops away from the village green as quickly as he can, without saying another word. Geoff Wade shouts after him, "I hate you! I hate you all," he says, feeling very unhappy about things.

Geoff stands alone by the side of the pond, still half dazed, while the ducks quack energetically behind him. Once he has regained his bearings, he trudges slowly away from the pond and the village green towards an old, thatched country cottage that stands further along the country lane down which the early-morning sport has just rode his horse.

Geoff lifts the latch of the gate to the cottage, still feeling the effects of last night's heavy session at the public house on the other side of the village. His mouth feels very dry indeed as he fumbles around for his keys inside his pockets and is almost surprised to find them still there.

He opens his front door then stumbles inside, almost tripping over the step that leads up into the hallway.

Once inside, Geoff slams the front door closed then makes his way towards the kitchen feeling very hungover and very angry at the same time. He puts his head under the cold tap in the kitchen, then drinks thirstily for what seems like an age to him. He finally turns the tap off, angrily throws off the soaking-wet, long brown overcoat that weighs so heavily on his back, then makes his way, plodding up the stairs, towards his bedroom.

Once he has stumbled into his bedroom, he slumps onto his bed in his wet clothes and quickly falls fast asleep. His heavy snoring soon fills the room where the half-closed curtains let the sun peek in through the gaps.

In what seems like an instantaneous moment for Geoff but is, in fact, almost an hour later, his alarm clock sounds loudly on the bedside table next to him. Geoff reluctantly wakes again from his hungover stupor and forces open his eyes. He sits up on his bed and stares at the open door with his bloodshot red eyes, forced wide open, just in case they close again for good.

Geoff can feel only anger for being woken yet again. "No! No! No! No! No!" declares Geoff, making his head hurt each time he says it. He turns to read seven o'clock on the alarm clock next to his bed, then slams his fist into it, knocking it from one side of the room to the other to make it shut up.

Geoff rubs his sore head and slowly remembers the very heavy session he got involved with in the nearby public house the evening before. He opens and closes his eyes as normally as he can until he realises where he is, what time it is, and where he should be. He collapses back onto his bed again, when all these questions have been answered in his head.

Chapter 2

Geoff strides away from his parked car with an old satchel in one hand. He trudges along the path that leads towards the bustling secondary school, Honibridge Modern, situated in the small market town of Honibridge in the very southernmost county of England.

He looks surprisingly neat and tidy given his early-morning antics only a few hours before and a shower seems to have washed away some of the effects of the booze he consumed in large quantities the night before. However, Geoff does not feel as well as he looks and he bows his head to avoid any unwanted company he may attract now that he approaches the entrance to the school.

The school bell rings noisily as Geoff turns into the grounds. Children dash past him to get through the school gates in time, where Geoff immediately happens upon the tall and stern gaze of one of his maths-teaching colleagues, Kenneth Jackson, who stands with his arms folded looking disapprovingly at all of the latecomers rushing past him, trying to avoid his attention.

Geoff does not try to run past his colleague, probably because he can't; probably because he'd rather have the day off today; and probably because he doesn't want to run into any of the other staff for as long as possible, but he would have preferred not to have run into Kenneth Jackson the day after one of his heavy sessions because Kenneth can be as unsympathetic about such matters as one can be.

It is then that Geoff remembers he has forgotten to shave and up close it must be instantly noticeable to the ever-observant Kenneth. He can feel the heavy stubble on his face and he's sure Kenneth will instantly put two and two together and realise what his colleague, Geoff Wade, has been up to the night before. He feels he really can't face Kenneth or any of the other teachers today and it makes him stop in his tracks and think about turning around and going home; that is until one of his students almost runs into him.

"Morning, sir," says one of his Year Eleven students, Ben Andrews, almost crashing into him on his way into the school. Geoff bows his head and pretends he didn't hear him but Andrews stands in front of him waiting for a reply, so Geoff feels forced to say something. At first no words come to mind and his mouth feels so dry that he's sure he won't be able to say anything, even if he tried, but he finally manages to utter a friendly greeting.

"Morning, Andrews," mutters Geoff, now quite sure he will be unable to say anything more. Andrews turns, dodges past him, then jumps through the gates into the school, still under the disapproving eye of Kenneth Jackson, until he disappears from the two teachers' sight.

Geoff then trudges through the gates into the school feeling sure he's the last one to pass Kenneth Jackson's stern gaze that morning. Kenneth is a fellow teacher, yet he still receives a disapproving look from his colleague. Geoff and the other teachers have become quite used to this over the years, so he smiles towards Kenneth and then trudges past him, hoping against hope that his colleague does not speak to him. Luckily for Geoff, on this occasion, he doesn't.

Geoff can still feel Kenneth's eyes boring into his back as he passes, so he turns his head and tries to smile at him again as he walks into the school. However, it doesn't quite come off a second time so Geoff picks up his walking speed and disappears into the bowels of the establishment, glad that he has avoided receiving a detention from the ever-watchful Mr. Jackson.

Geoff walks through the glass-surrounded corridor towards his classroom, summoning up as much energy as he can for the day ahead. He strides briskly into the classroom, then throws his satchel onto his desk as he surveys the eager students seated ahead of him. He opens his satchel, pulls out a maths text book, then checks that the students seated in front of him are those he's supposed to be teaching.

He then turns his back on them for a long while, so as to compose himself somewhat before they notice his bloodshot eyes, which of course they already have. His older students are all well aware of Mr Wade's looks and behaviour after a heavy session the night before. He is fortunate today that a few of them feel sorry for him, amongst the general quiet giggling that emanates from the rest of his students.

"Is it Pythagoras today, sir?" asks Ernest Thompson, trying to give Mr Wade some clue as to what he should be teaching them.

Geoff keeps his back to them while he flicks through his maths text book, then immediately goes to the pages on Pythagoras, now very thankful that one of his students has helped him out.

Ben Andrews, on the other side of the classroom, feels he should try and help Mr. Wade out, too. "Yes, sir, you promised we'd be starting Pythagoras today," he adds.

"No, I didn't," replies Geoff, testing them with his back still facing them.

"Oh, but sir, you did say last Friday that we would be starting Pythagoras today," pipes up Sarah Jordan from the back of the classroom.

"I say a lot of things," replies Geoff, still not convinced that the subject he should be teaching them is Pythagoras. Geoff rattles his brains for a moment. Is it really Pythagoras for Year Eleven, first period on Tuesday morning?

Geoff feels his dry mouth with his tongue until a thought finally pops into his head to confirm that it could well be Pythagoras for Year Eleven, first thing Tuesday. He finally turns around to face his students. His Year Eleven pupils look at him, all knowing how and why Geoff feels the way he does this fine and sunny spring morning.

"Pythagoras?" asks Geoff.

"Pythagoras, sir," replies Andrews.

Geoff writes Pythagoras on the board behind his desk, still feeling the effects of last night's booze. His actions make Geoff stumble, his head feels dizzy and he then feels quite sick. He suddenly feels forced to bound over to the window, open it hurriedly, then almost wretch onto the shrub garden below, while his students look on slightly shocked. They have never seen Mr Wade do that before.

Geoff forgets about his students for a moment with his head stuck out of the window. The fresh air makes him feel instantly better until he notices a pair of large eyes look at him from inside the classroom on the other side of the quad.

Rose Daniels, with long, flowing blonde hair and large eyes, looks at him with horror from across the quad. Geoff cannot take his eyes off her, despite Rose shaking her head at him and making a disgusted look on her face at the same time.

She hastily removes her gaze from him, knowing all too well why he is behaving the way he is and returns to show her class something on the board behind her.

Geoff comes round. He realises where he is, so he withdraws his head from outside, closes the window, then turns to face his Year Eleven students, still looking very white indeed.

His students all look back at him, not quite sure what to say or do until Sarah Jordan breaks the stony silence.

"You don't look too well, sir. Perhaps you should go and see the school nurse?" says Sarah.

Most of the other students begin to laugh as Geoff takes to his chair behind his desk.

"I feel worse than I look," replies Geoff.

"Surely that's not possible, sir?" retorts Thompson.

"For perhaps the first time this term, Thompson, you could well be right. Class, get on with your Pythagoras; I'll be back in a minute," says Geoff, already turning the knob on the classroom door to leave.

"But we haven't even started Pythagoras yet, sir," says Andrews.

"Don't be flippant, Andrews," says Geoff, slowly closing the door to the classroom behind him, still feeling very sick.

Geoff rushes along the corridor towards the toilet at the other end. On his journey there he sees the last person he would ever want to see anywhere in the world walk slowly towards him. Max Heckton, smartly dressed in a tweed jacket and cords, with a small manicured beard on his chin, soon changes his walking pace when he notices Geoff rushing towards him. He's delighted by the possible chance of an approaching confrontation with one of the many teachers he despises at the school.

Max eyes him angrily as Geoff quickly approaches. Geoff is feeling too unwell to notice Max's angry eyes or to change direction and walk the other way, which is what he would normally have done if he had seen Heckton approach him, so instead, Geoff walks briskly around him, hoping Heckton has more important business on his mind than to confront him in the corridor so early in the school day.

However, Max is in no mood to let Geoff just ignore him. He is relishing the chance of a possible confrontation with the one teacher in the school with whom he knows he could get into a serious confrontation. He can see Wade does not look well, so Heckton thrusts Geoff towards the side of the corridor, then pins his head to the wall and begins to emit a strange hissing sound into his face.

Geoff almost wretches once more because of Heckton's sudden attack. There's something scary in Heckton's expression as he makes his strange hissing sounds that makes Geoff move along the wall to get as far away from him as he can. Yet Heckton keeps him close by taking hold of his shirt collar and pushing him once more against the corridor wall. Geoff is feeling far too unwell to fight back or wrestle himself free and dare not even ponder what Heckton will do to him now that he has got him where he wants him.

"What have you done with Year Nine's geography books, Wade?" asks Heckton nastily. "Where have you hidden them?"

"I don't know what you're talking about, Max," replies Geoff.

"I know it must have been you who took them from my cupboard. Who else would have done such a thing?" says Heckton angrily.

"I still don't know what you're talking about, and I don't like your accusations, Heckton. You let me go this instant or I will flip you. I will flip you away," replies Geoff, now unable to stop himself getting angry despite the way he is feeling.

Heckton releases his grip on Geoff's tie. He is a little taken aback by Geoff's anger and his very pale-looking face. "Are you all right?" asks Heckton, releasing his grip on Geoff's arm and moving backwards away from him.

Geoff straightens his tie and regains his composure now that Heckton has taken a step backwards.

"If you don't return those geography books by lunch time, I will inform the headmaster. You got that, Wade?" adds Heckton menacingly.

Geoff has a sudden rush of blood to his head. He kicks Heckton's legs from under him making him fall to the floor. He is about to make a threatening remark to

Heckton, now that he has him on the ground, but Geoff cannot say anything else because he suddenly feels the nearby toilet beckon him hastily away.

Geoff bursts through the toilet door and lunges towards a toilet cubicle, then pukes loudly into the pan. He stands there for a moment with relief, then quickly convinces himself, for the time being, that he will never touch another drop of alcohol for as long as he lives.

A nervous boy in the cubicle next door dashes out of the toilet when he hears Geoff's antics on the other side of the partition. Geoff finally opens his cubicle door when it all sounds quiet on the other side. He approaches the mirror on the wall ahead of him, straightens his shirt and jumper, then looks into his bloodshot eyes. "And that is how we do things around this place," says Geoff satisfyingly and worryingly to himself.

Chapter 3

About half an hour later, Rose Daniels, the English teacher who saw Geoff's head out of the window from the other side of the quad earlier, walks heavy-footed towards the classroom door at the end of the corridor. She looks through the window in the door towards Geoff sitting behind his desk in front of his Year Eleven maths class. There's a detailed Pythagoras diagram on the white board behind him and a quiet class of students getting on with their work in front of him. She looks back towards Geoff.

Geoff sits at his desk in a kind of daydream while he thinks about dropping Year Nine's geography books into a fiercely burning fire at the bottom of his garden. Geoff chuckles to himself as the door to his classroom slowly opens.

Rose Daniels stands in the doorway of the classroom looking sternly towards him. Geoff looks lovingly back towards her as he gets up from his chair. No words are exchanged as he approaches. She gestures him out of the classroom, then closes the classroom door quietly behind them both.

"Geoff, you do not look well," says Rose.

"You're not the first to say so this morning, as it happens," replies Geoff.

"There are too many mornings when I'm saying the same thing to you, again and again. And this little episode out of the window just now, do you want everyone to turn against you? Why can't you pull your act together?" asks Rose, noticing that his heavy stubble and bloodshot eyes look as bad as she has ever seen them.

"I've got two tickets to the Bricklayers Arms for tonight. If you're not there, you may well see a repeat performance from me tomorrow morning," pleads Geoff.

Rose feels so disgusted by his attitude that she walks away from him without saying another word. Geoff looks longingly towards her back as she walks away. He feels heartbroken.

He composes himself as best he can, feeling the way he does, then opens the classroom door. Geoff now looks unhappy, as well as pale and sickly, as he retakes his seat behind his desk. He looks towards his students to find most of them looking at him questioningly, as well as feeling a little concerned for themselves at the same time. He opens a text book to hide his face from their glaring eyes.

Later that evening Rose Daniels accompanies Roger Little, an English teacher at the same school, to the local bowls club. Roger looks quite frail and small compared to the robust and healthy-looking woman in her early forties walking by his side.

"I heard about Geoff today, Rose. He's got a problem," says Roger Little.

"Yeah, I know," replies Rose, putting her arm through his as he leads her inside.

"He's absolutely no way over you, you do know that, don't you?" says Roger, opening an inside door for her. "He should make a change. Try another school," he adds, as they enter the plush surroundings of the very popular local bowls club.

"Maybe. You could be right; it's up to him though," replies Rose, as Roger leads her through the busy bowling-club crowd towards a loud, deeply tanned and charismatic-looking man standing at the bar of the lounge and dressed in very clean and crisp bowls-players' whites.

Malcolm Purdy watches them approach and greets them heartily when they reach the bar. Rose immediately notices the gold rings that cover almost all of his fingers. Purdy thrusts two glasses of wine at the pair of them when they reach him, almost spilling the contents over Rose's and Roger's rather frumpy-looking clothes in comparison to Malcolm's quite fetching get up.

"Welcome, Roger, I'm glad you've changed your mind. This must be the new recruit?" says Purdy, smiling a teeth-filled yet cold-looking grin at Rose.

"I felt I should make more time for my bowling. I've convinced myself that I can fit it into my busy schedule," says Roger, chuckling to himself.

Purdy remains stony-faced with no hint of a smile at Roger's attempt to lighten things up. Instead, Purdy brushes his crisp, white bowls shirt as he waits for Roger to shut up.

"This is Rose. She's played before, somewhere up north, I think," adds Roger.

"Have you, Rose? That is good to hear. Although we welcome complete novices too, of course. We have the time and we have the technology to cater for all types at this bowls club," says Purdy with a teethy smile.

"It was a few years ago now but I did get rather good, if I do say so myself," replies Rose.

"That is most interesting to hear," says Purdy.

"I was telling Rose in the car that this bowls club is apparently thought of as one of the most popular and sophisticated in the country, according to Malcolm," says Roger.

"Considered by some to be perhaps *the* premier bowls club in the country. Although there would be many a heated argument over that statement," replies Purdy, polishing off his pint of beer in one large gulp.

"Sophisticated bowls club?" asks Rose.

"I beg your pardon?" replies Purdy.

"You've said that this is the most sophisticated bowls club in the country?" asks Rose, more specifically.

"Sophisticated? This bowls club? Oh yes, absolutely it is. You only have to look at me to know how sophisticated we are here." replies Purdy.

"Now, let me show you the all-important bowls green, Rose," adds Purdy, leading them through the crowded lounge towards a huge, glass frontage that overlooks an immaculate-looking, floodlit, bowls green outside.

The green is full of late-middle-aged bowls players dressed in gleaming white outfits, all looking as though they are taking the game very seriously indeed.

Purdy smiles proudly as Roger and Rose look through a deeply tinted glass frontage towards the bowls players outside. "We are and have always been a very competitive bowls club. I'm sure Roger has told you that, Rose," he says.

Rose struggles to see the bowls players outside through the thickly tinted glass frontage but does not say anything about it to Purdy.

"Now, Roger, I know that you have played on this hallowed ground before and let me say this, Rose: we are delighted that Roger has made the time for us because his knowledge of the game has even impressed many of us battle-hardened club players," says Purdy to a captivated Rose.

"I took a liking to the game the first time I played, too," replies Rose, who can't wait to get out onto the bowls green to roll some balls.

"I can sense you would like a game, Rose. Let's see what I can arrange," says Purdy, looking around the busy lounge for signs of his second-in-command, as loud applause wafts through the half-open door in the far corner of the room.

"I noticed that new little Porsche you've parked in the car park last time you were here, Roger," says Purdy.

"Not so little, Malcolm. It's the most powerful one they make these days," replies Roger.

"There's a real throbbing under the bonnet isn't there, Roger?" says Rose excitedly. "It leaves all of the other cars standing when he puts it through its paces, doesn't it? You should see him overtake on a dual carriageway. It's a really powerful machine."

"You can say that again. It sometimes even scares me," replies Roger.

"Oh, you've got it well under control, Roger. I know you can handle it. I know you can handle its engine's throbbing power," adds Rose to a surprisingly interested Malcolm Purdy.

"This glass frontage must have set you back a few bob, Malcolm. There's a slight tint to the glass, isn't there?" says Roger interestedly.

Purdy fumes to himself. He's heard far too much talk about this very expensive, tinted-glass frontage that they are all looking through. He had questioned the tinted glass when they first installed it, last year, but the installers kept on telling him a regular glass frontage with no tint would have cost him double the price, which the club couldn't afford, so he was forced to stick with the tinted version. But how he had wished he hadn't, now that almost every visiting team player comments on the tinted-glass frontage and how difficult it is to see through it to the bowls green outside, especially at night.

Of course, he doesn't say anything to Rose and Roger about it, but Rose notices Purdy's face redden because of the consternation the tinted-glass frontage makes him feel every time it's mentioned. She watches Purdy begin to play agitatedly with the large gold ring on his left middle finger, so she says nothing further on the subject.

"Perhaps Roger has informed you of our success? We're county champions for the second year in a row and we're gearing up to make it three years back to back," says Purdy.

"Yes, Roger has told me. Roger's very competitive, too, in everything he does. You wouldn't think it to look at him. So he should fit into your competition team very well," replies Rose.

"And that's the key, Rose: it's a team effort, this game. We're lifelong players at this club. We've known each other for many years. That's partly what makes us as good as we are," says Purdy. "You'd both be joining a winning team if you were to start playing with us," he adds.

Purdy has taken an instant liking to Rose. He can immediately sense that she is as good at bowls as she has modestly said she is. He begins to introduce her and Roger to more of the crisply white-dressed bowl players, looking through the tinted-glass frontage towards the highly competitive matches being played under the floodlights outside.

After more introductions and more drinks, Rose soon feels quite tipsy, so it is left to the strictly sober Roger to continue to discuss the finer points of the game with a steely-eyed, white-haired lady nearby as Rose looks for a chair to sit on.

When she can't find a spare seat nearby, she is about to ask Roger for some help, when she notices something through the deeply tinted glass frontage outside. There's something happening out there that upsets the peace and calm of the competitive bowls matches and which soon causes several of the lady players to begin screaming.

A large and unkempt, hairy, drunken monster of a man lunges over the immaculate bowls green holding what could have been, to all intents and purposes, a spear. The drunken man shakes the spear angrily, which actually turns out to be a spade, towards the deeply tinted glass frontage of the bowls clubhouse on the other side of the bowls green.

With tears rolling down his cheeks, Geoff starts to throw some of the large chunks of bowls-green lawn he's dug up towards the bowls clubhouse where Rose looks on from inside, open-mouthed with shock. He can tell it is Rose inside the club house even through the tinted glass because of her big and wild hair. Geoff then watches a stray bowl roll towards him then drop into a hole in the green he's made by his angry digging.

"A hole in one!" shouts Geoff towards the clubhouse.

The other bowls players quickly retreat from him as fast as they can to leave Geoff take centre stage under the powerful floodlights and carry on throwing chunks of the bowls lawn at any one who moves close to him.

He can see Roger and Rose through the glass frontage on the opposite side of the bowls green, with drinks in their hands, and this makes him feel even more miserable. It causes more tears to roll down his cheeks.

It doesn't take long for several of the younger male bowls players to emerge from the darkness and surround Geoff. They approach him cautiously but purposely. Geoff can see them approach so he holds his ground as best he can. He shakes his spade angrily at all of them to try and ward them off but the surrounding bowls players have weighed him up and have decided to tackle him.

Inside the bowls club, Rose, Roger and Purdy look on with horror at Geoff's antics on the other side of the tinted-glass frontage. Rose knows Geoff's drinks evening at The Bricklayers Arms has got out of hand, as she knew it would do, but she's still surprised to see him here at the bowls club this evening.

Rose still hasn't quite managed to focus on Geoff properly because of the many brandies she has consumed and she's still hoping that she has been mistaken and that the hairy ape outside on the bowls green lawn is not Geoff but some disgruntled or rejected bowls player from the club. It takes Roger to confirm her worst fears.

"Isn't that Geoff, Rose? Isn't it?" Roger gets closer to the glass. "Yes, I'm sure that's Geoff Wade. He's a maths teacher at our school, you know," says Roger to Malcolm Purdy quite excitedly.

"Oh, no, Geoff!" cries out Rose through the soundproofed, tinted-glass frontage. "What are you doing?" she adds, feeling completely distressed.

Outside on the vandalised bowls green lawn Geoff still digs furiously into the manicured turf with his spade, despite the surrounding bowls players closing in on him. He can hear a few muffled and distressed cries and shrieks from inside the bowls club and he hopes against hope that Rose is one of those making them, which she is.

The surrounding male bowls players decide to tackle Geoff as one, so with a secret gesture made by one of them they all pile onto the top of him to quickly remove the spade from his hands. They then jump on top of him to try and stop him moving.

Geoff writhes and struggles for a moment. His anger and hurt is acute but the combined strength of the half-dozen bowls players on top of him is finally enough to pin him to the ground.

Geoff raises his head and looks to the club house to see if Rose has taken an interest in his plight.

"Is this what you want me to do? Is this what you want me to do, Rose?" shouts Geoff in between sobs.

But Rose has stayed inside the clubhouse and Geoff can only imagine and hope that the women he can just about see through the tinted-glass frontage is indeed Rose. Geoff finally lowers his head to the ground to admit defeat.

Rose still looks on, open-mouthed, towards the captured hooligan lying on the bowls lawn outside. She doesn't notice Roger standing next to her, trying to stifle a grin: if she had, she might have slapped him across the face.

Malcolm Purdy, standing near to them, has watched the unfolding excitement outside with similar slack-jawed shock. His precious bowls green lies in ruins and Rose feels sure she will see Purdy thrust his gold-ring-covered fist straight through the tinted-glass frontage at any moment.

She would have been right had Purdy not heard the hooligan outside mention Rose's name. This makes him hold his fuming anger for a short moment until he can discover exactly what this is all about. So instead of slamming his fist through the glass frontage facing him, his fury continues behind his very red face and behind his wide and livid, bulbous eyes.

Once Purdy has seen the hooligan firmly held in check on the bowls green lawn, he dashes out of the clubhouse door, runs across the green towards the floored Geoff Wade lying on the grass, then unleashes a tirade of angry expletives that cannot be heard from inside the bowls club.

Roger Little grabs Rose by the arm and leads her out of the bowls club as quickly as he can, before anyone else finds out the connection between them and the floored hooligan outside.

With tears scalding her eyes, Rose slips into the passenger seat of Roger's powerful red Porsche parked proudly right outside the front door of the bowls club. As Roger jumps into the driving seat, two police cars speed over the gravel drive towards them with their blue lights flashing.

Roger certainly does not want to get involved with the police so he wheel-spins his Porsche hastily away along the other side of the gravel driveway, keen to avoid the fracas they've left behind them in the bowls club.

"I don't know what to say, Rose," says Roger, still trying to stifle a chuckle.

Rose looks towards Roger angrily. She sees Roger's smirking face and now knows only too well how Roger feels about the situation. "Don't say anything, Roger. I'm still too upset. Whatever was he thinking. . ?"

"I think there's a teacher at our school who needs to sort out some issues, Rose. And it certainly isn't me," says Roger, driving his Porsche out of the bowls club and onto a country lane.

"You think you're so perfect, don't you, Roger?" replies Rose with frustration.

"Well, I certainly don't go digging up my local bowls club lawn of a Tuesday evening," replies Roger, finally bursting into a chuckle.

Rose fumes. "You make me so angry, Roger," says Rose as their Porsche throbs along the winding lane. "You drive around in your Porsche thinking you're the best, you're the greatest. Well, I've got news for you. You're in no way whatsoever the greatest. You're not even the best English teacher in our school, let alone anywhere else."

"I say, that's a bit harsh, Rose. I do my best. I mark all my pupils' homework on time. I try to motivate as many of my students as I can. Which other English teacher at our school works as hard as me?" asks Roger, obviously hurt by her harsh words.

Rose can sense she's finally got to him. She calms down a little when she notices Roger's smirk finally disappear; that is until Roger gets back at her.

"You see? You still get so defensive whenever we talk about Geoff. And we still seem to be talking about him, even when he's not pulling stunts like the one he's just pulled," replies Roger.

Rose knows he's right. She remains quiet for a moment. "I'm sorry, Roger. I promise we'll never talk about Geoff again," she says finally.

"I thought we had agreed on that. And let me tell you, Rose – the headmaster will hear about this little prank Geoff has just pulled," Roger replies as he expertly corners his powerful machine along the country lane.

"No! No, Roger, let me talk to the headmaster about it. Please let me talk to him first. I've been meaning to have a little chat with him, anyway. You promise, Roger? You promise to let me talk to him first about this bowls club thing?" pleads Rose.

"As long as you're sure you will talk to him about it. I'm all for teachers' private lives remaining private but this little incident. . . well, it might reflect badly on the school," replies Roger.

"Yes, leave it to me, Roger. I'll talk to him first thing tomorrow morning," says Rose, now more worried about Geoff than she has ever been before.

Roger feels triumphant. Geoff could not have done anything better to alienate himself even more from Rose than what has just occurred at the bowls club. He accelerates his Porsche along a straight stretch of country lane with the engine's throbbing sounds echoing loudly through the trees and countryside all around them, long after the rear lights of his car have disappeared from view.

Chapter 4

Rose walks hurriedly towards the front door of a public house that sits nestled in a small valley in the surrounding countryside of Honibridge during her lunch break, several weeks later. The sun shines strongly as she makes her way inside. She is forced to stand still, just inside the public house, for a moment to allow her eyes to adjust to the darkness of the lounge bar that stretches out before her.

The pub is busy, being lunch time. She can see people sitting at tables and nibbling at food all around her but she cannot see the one person she is seeking. Then she looks towards the bar of the pub and immediately recognises the long brown overcoat that belongs to Geoff Wade.

She sidles over to the bar to find Geoff sitting inside the old overcoat he bought from a charity shop in his student days, almost two decades earlier, with a half-drunk pint of beer in front of him. She taps him on the shoulder at first. Geoff turns towards her. He tries to focus on her but struggles because he is so drunk. Rose isn't surprised to find Geoff in this state.

"I thought I might find you here, Geoff," says Rose.

"Ah, here she is. A friend in need is a friend who needs to be shopped to the headmaster," replies Geoff holding up his half-drunk pint glass to her.

Rose looks to the nervous-looking barman behind the bar. "How many has he had?" asks Rose.

"This is the third, my dear, of many. Well, that depends on whether you will be joining me. . ." says Geoff, gesturing to the barman to fix her a drink while Rose leans against an empty bar stool next to him.

"I left if for a long as I could, Geoff. I kept Roger from telling the headmaster about your behaviour but I had to tell him about that little incident at the bowls club. It made the papers. I couldn't keep it under wraps for any longer. It's not just Roger who's noticed you falling in standards, you know," says Rose, looking into Geoff's pink eyes.

"Well, I shall certainly have plenty of time to think about my past behaviour after being suspended for a month. Thanks a lot, Rose," replies Geoff, polishing off the rest of his beer then gesturing to the barman to refill his glass.

Rose sighs a deep sigh. "I knew this would happen, you see. That's why I left it for as long as I could. You'd end up in here in an even worse state than before," she says. "You must find other ways of dealing with your issues, Geoff. You can't just drink them away," adds Rose, looking at her watch. "I must get back now," she says, after trying to persuade the barman not to give Geoff any more drinks.

"Ah, yes, lucky you. Some of us still have jobs to get back to," replies Geoff, spilling some of his beer over his lap.

"You need help, Geoff. Are you going to get the help you need or will I have to arrange that for you, as well?" says Rose angrily to Geoff, as he turns away from her.

Rose can spend no more time with him when he's like this so she saunters back out of the pub leaving Geoff with a full glass of beer staring at him from the bar.

Geoff is used to Rose behaving like this, so he returns to his drinking as if Rose had never entered the public house in the first place. He then looks along the bar to the other end of the pub. There's a drunken, plumpish man sitting on a bar stool at the far end, leaning against the wall, and Geoff's sure he recognises him from somewhere.

Russell Appleby is dressed in a tweed jacket and a tight shirt that emphasises his plumpness even further. He knocks back scotches like there's no tomorrow.

"There's nothing like a pint to wipe away the cobwebs of a failed relationship," says Geoff to the drunken Appleby, who turns to notice him for the first time.

"Ah, yes, I'm sure," says Appleby raising his glass to Geoff. "Cheers," he adds.

"Appleby, isn't it?" says Geoff recognising his distinctive tweed jacket.

"Russell Appleby," replies Appleby.

"The farmer who owns most of the land around here?" says Geoff.

"It's my father who owns most of the land around here," replies Appleby.

"Ah yes, of course. That explains why you're in here so often. I thought I'd seen you here before," replies Geoff. "My name's Geoff. Geoff Wade. Teacher," he adds. Geoff then cracks up. "Funny how things turn out, isn't it?" he laughs.

"Funny indeed," replies Appleby.

"Another scotch for my friend, here," says Geoff, forcing the nervous barman to pour Appleby another scotch.

Several hours later, under a pale moon, Geoff sways and stumbles through some heavy undergrowth as he makes his way through a field. He trips in the darkness and falls face down into some mud. He lies there for a moment, blowing bubbles into the wet mud beneath his face, until a hand grabs his collar and lifts him to his feet.

Geoff and Appleby stagger on through the overgrown field until they're forced to negotiate a fence at the other end. They climb over the fence, then walk on through a field full of half-asleep bleating sheep that they cannot see in the darkness.

"I just get so bored sometimes. It's not the children. I can cope with the children. I actually enjoy teaching them. It's just. . . I need something to break the monotony sometimes. You know what I mean, Russell?" says Geoff.

"Not really, no. I don't. This way," replies Appleby.

"Russell, my pal. . ." says Geoff putting his arm around Russell's shoulders but then falling over a half hidden sheep. "What's that? Where are we?" says Geoff slightly concerned.

"It's okay, Geoff. I'm a farmer," replies Appleby.

"I bet you say that to all the sheep," replies Geoff. "The tweed jacket, Russ, I should have guessed."

Geoff finally notices a light glimmer through some trees ahead of them under the moonlight. Appleby leads Geoff through the trees towards the light shining out through the kitchen of his large farmhouse.

As they approach the kitchen door, Geoff can hear some more agitated animal noises through the darkness from somewhere nearby. They make him feel quite reticent to go inside.

"Russ, how far have we walked? Feels like I'm in the middle of nowhere," says Geoff.

Appleby fumbles with the lock on the kitchen door then finally opens it. They both stumble inside. Appleby immediately goes to the sherry bottle standing on the kitchen table and pours a glass for each of them.

"A glass of sherry, Geoff? I'd like you to try it," says Appleby, holding out the glass.

"I'm not much of a sherry drinker, Russell, my old fruit," replies Geoff, slumping into an old, comfortable chair in the corner of the large kitchen.

But Appleby seems most insistent Geoff try some of it, so he brings the bottle of homemade-looking sherry over to the chair. "Try a glass, Geoff, I insist. It's got a real sting to it. It'll warm you: it's still a bit nippy out there," he says, putting the glass into Geoff's hand.

Geoff grabs the sherry glass, then drinks the contents down in one gulp. "Nice place you've got here, Appleby," says Geoff, feeling the drink's warming effects.

"Well?" asks Appleby.

"Well, what?" replies Geoff.

"What do you think of the sherry?" asks Appleby again.

Geoff opens and closes his mouth to try and taste the sherry but he can't. "I'm sorry, Russ, I can't tell you if it's any good or not. Not much of a sherry drinker myself, old fruit," he replies, looking out of the nearby window into the starry darkness.

There is something that keeps Geoff's attention fixed on the window and the darkness outside. He's sure he can hear something in the darkness.

"Can you hear something, Russ? I'm sure there's something out there. I'm not sure what it is but I think you should take a look some time. It doesn't sound right," says Geoff, as Appleby leaves him alone in the kitchen for a moment.

Geoff gets up from his comfortable chair and stares out of the window into the darkness but only his drunken reflection stares back at him. He hastily puts down the empty sherry glass on the kitchen table, determined not to touch another drop of the stuff tonight.

The constant faint noise from outside really begins to annoy him. Geoff is sure he can hear a faint humming, so he puts his ear closer to the window to make sure he's not hearing things.

Just as he does so, Appleby returns to the kitchen. "You know, Appleby, I'm sure I can hear some kind of humming outside this window. Is your boiler on the blink? If it is, you need to get it seen to before it explodes or something," says Geoff turning to face him.

Geoff's mouth drops open at the sight that greets him. Appleby stands before him dressed from head to toe in a white bee-keepers outfit, complete with a netted head covering.

"What's going on, Russ?" asks Geoff manoeuvring himself towards the closed kitchen door.

"I told you, there's something I want to show you," replies Appleby, throwing a spare bee-keepers head-net towards him.

Geoff grabs the head covering out of the air. "Russ – bees, sheep, ducks, whatever animals you have got up here on your farm, they've got nothing to do with me. I know nothing about any of them. I'm no farmer," replies Geoff, getting slightly concerned.

"Put the net hat on," says Appleby throwing the one-piece, bee-keeper outfit towards Geoff.

Geoff picks up the all-in-one bee suit from the floor and finally puts two and two together. "Those are bees you're keeping outside there?" asks Geoff, looking out of the kitchen window once more.

"Yes, Geoff: bees, and lots of them," replies Appleby opening the kitchen door.

Geoff gets nervous about the whole thing – the bees, as well as being here in Appleby's farmhouse with a man who's gradually appearing to be quite mad to him. "I don't think so, Russ. I'm going nowhere near no bees; especially not tonight, being drunk and all," replies Geoff sensibly.

"I told you in the pub I needed your help," says Appleby.

"You didn't mention anything about bees. I'll get stung. Badly stung," says Geoff, throwing the bee-keepers suit back at him.

"There's a good chance you will get stung," says Appleby. "Joking, Geoff," he adds.

"Yes, and that's why I'm going nowhere near no bees tonight, or any other night for that matter," replies Geoff.

"It's what I brought you all the way here for," says Appleby. "And I did say there could be something in it for you, too," he adds.

"I don't feel well," says Geoff, feeling sick and about to throw inside his bee head-net.

"Come on, I'll lead the way," says Appleby.

"I can't," replies Geoff.

"From what you've told me in the pub, you've got nothing else to do for a while," says Appleby.

Geoff feels angry for some reason. He thinks about Rose. Then he thinks about his suspension, so he says, "You're right. Whatever you're getting me involved with better be worth my while, though. I don't like bees and I never have done," adds Geoff, as he tries drunkenly to put the bee suit on over his clothes.

Appleby eventually leads Geoff through a dark field under a star-filled sky. Both of them are dressed from head to toe in bee-keepers' clobber.

"I've been cross-breeding bees for years, Geoff," says Appleby, leading him deeper into a pitch-dark field. "I don't know why: my father's never had an interest in bees. Perhaps that's why," adds Appleby.

"I agree with your father. Rather you than me," replies Geoff.

"It's rather addictive, you know," says Appleby.

"I can think of better addictions," replies Geoff, looking back towards the lights of the farmhouse through the trees and ready to walk back towards them at the slightest inconvenience.

As the dark field stretches out before them, Geoff gradually begins to hear the humming bees that he heard in the farmhouse earlier. They seem to be getting louder, much louder, until they get close enough for the bees to hum a deep hum that almost seems to come from under the ground he stumbles over.

Appleby remains silent as they stumble onwards until Geoff can finally make out five, tall bee hives that stand ahead of him silhouetted under a pale moonlight.

Geoff stands still for a moment. He does not want to get any closer to the bees. Appleby's forced to pull him onwards.

"These bee-keepers suits will protect us, even from these beauties," says Appleby, slightly madly.

"What do you mean, even?" asks Geoff nervously.

"I've been breeding our humble bumble bee for years. Then a chance meeting guided me towards the Uruguayan bee, Geoff. I don't know why I didn't try it earlier – cross-breeding the Uruguayan with our very own humble bumble bee," informs Appleby, falling upon fairly deaf ears.

"What did you say, Appleby? I can't hear what you're saying. There's a terrible humming coming from somewhere," says Geoff, stumbling then falling onto the grass to somehow stop himself from going any nearer the very tall-looking bee hives silhouetted under the moon just ahead of him.

He leaves Appleby to approach the nearest bee hive by himself. He watches Appleby slowly remove the top cover and allow a swarm of large bees to take to the dark skies above him.

Geoff is scared by the swarming bees, so he stays rooted to the wet grass to keep a good distance between himself and Appleby. "Look at the size of those bees! I've never seen bees that size before," says Geoff, looking up from the ground to watch the enormous bees swarm around Appleby's head.

Appleby is forced to take quite a few steps backwards as the large bees try to sting him. Appleby gets worried. "You leave them alone, they'll leave you alone," says Appleby, wishing he'd never removed the top from the bee hive in his drunken state.

"That sounds like a good plan, Russell. Perhaps you should listen to what you have to say from time to time," replies Geoff, getting back to his feet then retreating a good few steps as he tries to avoid the bees swarming towards him. "You've disturbed them, Russ, and they're too big to be disturbed," adds Geoff.

"These are monster bees, Geoff. They're the product of my cross breeding the bumble bee with the Uruguayan bee. The queen is the size of a bap," says Appleby.

"A bap?" says Geoff, slightly concerned.

"The queen's the size of a bread bap, Geoff; a circular bread bap," says Appleby.

"That's big, isn't it? For a bee?" asks Geoff.

"One sting from her and you're a gonner," replies Appleby.

Geoff can almost see Appleby's wide, mad eyes inside his bee-keeper's head net, so he quickly stumbles back through the field towards the farmhouse. He's heard enough from Appleby and now he's seen enough.

Geoff can hear Appleby chuckle behind him as he waddles back towards the farmhouse. Appleby's chuckling causes the cover from the top of the bee hive to fall out of his gloved hands and crash to the ground. Appleby chuckles some more.

Geoff feels too scared to look back towards Appleby. His stumbling soon turns into a run because the deeply humming bees sound closer to him now than they did before.

"Where are you going, Geoff?" shouts Appleby through the darkness. "I wanted to show you these bees! You had to see them."

"I must be going, Russ. School tomorrow and all that," replies Geoff, now well out of Appleby's sight.

"I thought you said you were suspended?" says Appleby.

"I must have been lying or something," replies Geoff tripping over a mound in the hidden grass below him and falling flat on his face. Geoff picks himself up then gasps with shock, when he finds Russell Appleby standing above him holding an inner sliver of the bee hive with bees swarming all over it.

Geoff quickly fumbles his head net back over his head. "What are you doing, Appleby?" he says. "You're scaring me now: you've just said that these bees could sting us to death," adds Geoff feeling the honey drip from the inner sliver of the bee hive that Appleby holds in front of him onto the top of his head net.

"The point of all this cross breeding, Geoff, is not to produce very large bees. It's to produce this golden honey that I have dripping here from this very cover," says Appleby.

"Try telling that to the bees. All they're concerned with at the moment is that a large animal has just removed the roof of their house in the middle of the night as they're all trying to sleep," replies Geoff, sliding away from Appleby and the bees as best he can in the darkness.

As Geoff makes sure his bee suit covers every part of his body, Appleby bravely removes the thick glove from one of his hands then puts some of the honey onto his finger and puts it into his mouth, while the bees still hum loudly and continue to try to sting him.

"This honey is the best I have ever tasted and I am a connoisseur in such matters, Geoff," says Appleby. "You must taste some of it. There was some of this honey in my homemade sherry you tasted earlier," adds Appleby.

"There was? I couldn't taste it. I'm in no fit state to taste it and I'm certainly no honey connoisseur," replies Geoff. "I really must be going," he adds.

"This is probably some of the finest honey ever made and let me tell you, I've tasted many types of honey from all around the world," says Appleby, helping himself to some more of the honey and completely ignoring the bees that sting his unprotected hand.

"Yes, I'll take your word for it, Russ. You seem to have a keen interest in these little blighters. I'm just glad it's as dark as it is so that I can't see so many of the damn things," replies Geoff.

"Here, you must try some of this honey on its own, straight from the bee hive. I need a second opinion. How does it taste to you?" says Appleby, dripping some of the honey into Geoff's mouth.

"Yak! That is far too strong. That can't be honey! You've cross-bred some new kind of stuff here. Yak!" says Geoff.

"You know, you could be closer to the truth than you think. It's certainly the strongest honey I've ever tasted, I'm sure of it," says Appleby.

"Here, let me try some more of that," says Geoff, opening his mouth. Appleby drips some more of the honey into Geoff's mouth, despite the buzzing bees all around them.

"Ouch!" cries Geoff.

"What – it's that good?" asks Appleby excitedly.

"A bee just stung me," replies Geoff, tasting the strong honey at the same time. He gestures to Appleby to drip more of the honey into his mouth until Appleby feels he's had enough of the stuff.

"That's enough," says Appleby, as Geoff slips on the wet grass and falls down because of the strong-tasting honey. "Are you feeling all right?"

"That's hit the spot," replies Geoff, getting back to his feet while ignoring the stinging bees.

"This honey taste is strong: it's going to affect you," says Appleby, now walking back towards the bee hive to replace the inner cover and taking most of the hovering bees back with him.

"Yes, I believe it will," says Geoff, feeling unusually reinvigorated and strangely as sober as he's felt for months. "You know what? I already feel better than I've felt for ages," he says into the darkness.

Geoff breathes in deeply. He shakes his arms free, then has a sudden desire to run and run hard. Geoff runs as fast as he can through the field, under a pale moon, for perhaps the first time since his school days and he doesn't want to stop. It was never one of his favourite activities, even at school, but now he runs and runs and runs and never feels out of breath.

He quickly reaches the other end of the field and feels ready to run all the way back. He can just about see the outline of the tall bee hives on the other side of the field and he realises he has just run all the way across a very large field indeed with no problem at all.

Geoff breathes in deeply once more. Now he's filled with a desire to jump, as well, so he starts to run then jump as high as he can once he has picked up speed. Mid-way through one jump, he takes a look at the ground below to find it some way beneath him. His jumps have turned into enormous leaps into the sky and Geoff can't quite believe it at first. In fact, he feels quite uneasy about it because he's never been one for heights, so he decides to slow and come to a halt in the middle of the field to get a grip on things.

Once he's convinced himself that he's experiencing the effects of Appleby's honey, he turns away from the bee hives just ahead of him and runs in the opposite direction towards a field further away. His jumps become higher and further and he feels completely exhilarated, as well as intoxicated, by the experience. He makes enormous leaps through the field, under a pale moon, that no one else has ever made before him.

Geoff finally slows and stops in the middle of an unfamiliar field, when the outline of a small hamlet appears ahead. He breathes in heavily yet he still feels no tiredness or breathlessness. "I was never this fit, even at school," says Geoff to himself.

He looks backwards into the darkness but just as he expects, there's no sign of Appleby or the bee hives now. He's left them miles behind him. He realises he has no clue as to his whereabouts, so he decides to jump on in great leaps towards the hamlet ahead, so as to get his bearings.

In the hamlet, nestled between two small undulating hills under a pale moon, there's a house at the very edge of the fields and on the outside window of an upstairs bedroom of this house there's a faint tap, tap, tap, that disturbs the two sleeping inhabitants inside.

Rose rouses in the bed. She pulls her arm away from Roger who is lying next to her, then sleepily turns to look out of the window to find out what the tapping noise could be. She sees no one there: it's still dark, so she rolls over and goes back to sleep.

But the annoying tapping sound does not go away. The tapping actually gets louder, forcing Rose awake again. She opens one eye to look out of the window and to her absolute horror, she sees Geoff's wide-eyed face appear outside the window for a moment, then disappear.

Rose sits quickly upright in her bed. It can't be Geoff, can it? She ponders. Not even Geoff would be calling around at this hour, surely not? While she ponders, she continues to look out of the window for more signs of him.

Then, to her further horror, Geoff appears outside her window again. His face is wide eyed and quite excitable as he taps again on her window with his fingers. He then disappears from view once more.

"Oh, no, it's Geoff!" says Rose, shaking Roger awake at the same time. "Roger?" she insists.

Roger finally stirs, then tries to turn away from her. Rose is forced to get out of bed to investigate for herself. She puts her dressing gown on as Roger opens an eye.

"What is it, Rose?" asks Roger.

"It's Geoff. Did you leave a ladder out last night?" asks Rose, moving towards the window.

"Geoff Wade? How does he know where I live? The headmaster will hear about this first thing tomorrow morning, Rose," says Roger sitting up in his bed, feeling alarmed.

"Oh, shut up, Roger," says Rose walking out of the bedroom, while putting her slippers on.

Rose descends the stairs, then opens the front door directly ahead of her. She finds Geoff jumping as high as the house, then back down to earth again.

"This is getting serious, Geoff. What are you doing?" she asks.

"You tell me," says Geoff excitedly, as he jumps up to the bedroom window again to look at Roger lying in his bed, fast asleep once more.

"What has happened to you this time?" asks Rose, when he lands again in front of her. Geoff stands in front of her looking excited and invigorated like never before. Then Geoff laughs at her.

"I'm serious, Geoff. Roger's getting hassled and stressed by you like never before since your suspension. It's been really hard work keeping him calm and sweet and then you pull another stunt like this one, tonight," says Rose looking into Geoff's eyes for answers.

"Poor Roger," replies Geoff.

"You know I don't like to see Roger getting hassled. You know what he's like. Any chance to shop you to the headmaster. This time he'll have more ammunition, you disturbing his sleep like this," says Rose. "If he does tell the headmaster, I expect it'll be the last time you'll teach at our school," she adds.

"They won't let me back there, anyway. I know it," says Geoff, finally feeling the honey's effects fade a little. "The headmaster's never really been on my side, and with Roger around. . ."

"The headmaster – he's on your side as well as Roger's. You've got three weeks left of your suspension. I suggest you keep yourself out of trouble. The headmaster likes you more than you think, he's told me. You're popular with the children. We'll be able to get him on your side but as long as you stay out of trouble. You must calm down. Do you know what that means?" says Rose, as she watches Geoff jump as high as the house again.

Rose sighs one of her well-known, deep sighs. She knows it'll be near impossible for Geoff to stay out of trouble, when he's been hurt like this – and this suspension has really hurt him. Geoff stops jumping for a moment.

"You've got to move on, Geoff. We finished ages ago, unhappily, I seem to remember. I'm with Roger now and we're blissfully happy together," says Rose.

"Noticed anything about me? Anything unusual?" asks Geoff.

"You're as rat-arsed as usual for a Tuesday night – a school night – so nothing unusual. In fact, all very usual for you. And another thing: Roger's not going to be happy you know where he lives. How did you find out?" replies Rose.

"I'm not happy Roger's sleeping with my wife," says Geoff.

"I'm not your wife any more, Geoff. We're best off apart and away from each other. You've got to get over this. Roger's been as patient as he can be. He's not going to stand for it much longer if you keep on hassling us like this," pleads Rose.

"To hell with Roger," says Geoff angrily.

Rose can't stand any more of Geoff's angry rantings, so she slams the front door closed in his face. Geoff turns away from the slammed door with tears in his eyes. He's not going to bother her any more tonight, so he jumps high and far back through the fields into the darkness.

Rose looks out through the window in the front door towards Geoff jumping away in large leaps through the fields. She finally turns away from the door when she can no longer see him. Confusion lines appear on her forehead as tears well up in her eyes.

"Yes, that is a bit unusual – even for you, Geoff," she says to herself.

Chapter 5

Geoff's mobile phone beeps on his bedside table as the sun shines brightly through the edges of the curtains, where he failed to close them properly the night before. He stirs slowly, then sits upright in his bed.

He is as white as a sheet and his eyes are as bloodshot as can be. He quickly lies back down on his bed, slamming his fists into the bed mattress beside him. "No, no, no, no, no, no!" groans Geoff angrily, feeling very hungover. He looks to his bedside clock. It's eleven o'clock in the morning. Geoff throws back his duvet and jumps out of bed.

Geoff drives his car slowly along the road outside his school. He can see several of the teachers already walking towards their cars inside the school car park at the beginning of lunch break.

Geoff looks in the rear-view mirror at his hungover face. He wonders about driving back home immediately but he has taken so much trouble to be here, even at this late hour, that he continues onwards.

He can see the teachers look at him as he drives slowly past. Some of them just peer through the fence towards him, while others make half smiles at him that

Geoff's keen to avoid, so he puts his hand next to his face to try and hide himself from the teachers' peering and smiling faces. He has no intention of going into the school today.

Inside the headmaster's office on the third floor, overlooking the front of the school, the headmaster, Anthony Bright, mid-fifties, tall but youthful, peers through the window blinds towards Geoff driving his car along the road outside. Geoff's battered old car draws attention wherever it goes. Bright quickly lets the window blind swing back again, once he's seen Geoff avoid turning into the school car park. Bright then returns to his desk looking very concerned about something or other.

Outside the school, inside Geoff's battered noisy old car, he finally spots Rose walking out of the school gates ahead of him. He drives alongside her, then winds down the passenger window. He looks towards Rose with his bloodshot eyes and unwashed, unkempt hair.

"Rose, Rose!" says Geoff, leaning towards the open passenger window.

Rose keeps on walking towards her car, trying her best to ignore him. She walks faster. Geoff speeds up his car to keep up with her.

"I know where he keeps his honey! Last night, Rose – I know where Russell Appleby keeps his honey!" shouts Geoff, as Rose fumbles around in her handbag for her car keys. She quickly slopes into her car, still ignoring him as best she can, then slams her car door closed. Geoff drives on past her.

Ten minutes later, Rose drives her car into the library car park and it's not long after that when Geoff parks his car right next to hers. Rose stares at him angrily from inside her car.

Geoff jumps out of his car, then appears by her window. Rose has a good mind to start her car again and drive away but she can see several other cars blocking her escape route in her car mirror. She reluctantly winds down her window.

"I know where he keeps his honey!" says Geoff excitedly, again.

"What? What are you talking about, Geoff?" says Rose, grabbing some library books form the passenger seat.

"I know where Russell Appleby keeps his honey. Or, at least, I'm pretty sure I know," replies Geoff, beginning to sweat.

Rose looks towards the scruffy-looking Geoff standing outside her car window and begins to wonder if he has started to lose his mind, as well.

"Geoff – Roger spoke to the headmaster about you coming round to his house last night. Sorry, I couldn't stop him this time," says Rose, still not sure whether she wants to get out of the car.

"It is none of the headmaster's business what I do outside school," replies Geoff.

Rose sighs. "The headmaster's trying to stay as neutral as possible on the matter, from what I can gather, but Roger's had about enough from you. Anywhere or any time he can get you into trouble, he will do so from now on, I'm afraid," says Rose to an unwell-looking Geoff. "So you have been warned. I can't protect you from him any longer," she adds.

Geoff opens the door to her car to allow Rose to get out. "The headmaster's not going to review your suspension kindly if you carry on like this. Get it into your head, will you?" says Rose, as she drops one of her library books that Geoff instantly picks up from the ground.

"The headmaster can take a running jump. Maybe I don't want to go back to his lousy school, anyway," says Geoff as they walk together towards the library.

"I'm saying this for your own sake. Stay out of the game. Lay low for a while, like you are supposed to do with a suspension," replies Rose sensibly.

"I need your help, Rose. I think you're the only one who can help me now," says Geoff.

"You need more than my help," replies Rose.

Geoff soon realises how he must look to Rose and knows he's got some work to do to bring her round to his way of seeing things. "Okay, Rose. I'll try and do as you say. How about one more drink for old times' sake? I'll turn things around, I promise," says Geoff, looking pleadingly into her eyes.

Rose sighs. "You promise you'll get help? That you'll call someone this afternoon? That you'll stay quiet until your suspension is over?" replies Rose.

"I promise I will do everything you say, Rose," says Geoff, opening the door to the library for her.

"I'm with Roger now, Geoff, and we're blissfully happy together. And take a bath before you go anywhere next time," replies Rose, holding her nose.

Geoff gives her a salute, then walks forlornly back towards his battered old car. He gets in, then checks his mirror to look at his unwashed greasy hair and bloodshot eyes.

Later that evening, Geoff brings two drinks over to their table inside the Bricklayers Arms. The pub is busy and Geoff recognises a couple of other teachers from their school, drinking at the bar. He nods towards them to acknowledge them, but they look only disapprovingly back towards him, despite his now cleanly washed and shaven appearance.

Geoff sits at the table and knocks back a pint of beer in one big gulp. "So, did you see me last night, or what?" he says, sitting opposite Rose, who can't quite escape the stern gaze of the other two teachers standing not far away from them.

"It was three in the morning when you kindly woke me up. I was in no mood for your antics at three in the morning. I'm in no mood for your antics at any other time for that matter," replies Rose, supping on a glass of wine.

"Russell Appleby's got some honey. He crossbreeds bees you know. That's what I was trying to tell you at lunch time," says Geoff, pulling a funny face at the two teachers at the bar.

"Roger's got a Porsche? Did you know?" replies Rose.

"You're not seriously suggesting that Roger's Porsche impresses you more than Appleby's honey?" says Geoff.

"What are you talking about, Geoff?" replies Rose.

"Appleby's stumbled onto something with his honey. Didn't you see me last night? That's what I'm trying to say," replies Geoff. "I'm sure he keeps his honey in that barn right next to his kitchen. It'll be tricky, the barn being near to the kitchen back door and all, but it'll only be a few jars," says Geoff, getting ready to go to the bar for a refill.

"I still don't know what you're talking about and I'm sure it means you're going to do exactly the opposite of what I have said you should do," says Rose, almost ready to get up and walk out of the pub.

"I would normally listen to your advice, as you know, but this honey of his. . . We've got to know his secret. I jumped through those fields in only a few large leaps last night," says Geoff, keeping his voice as quiet as possible. "Didn't you see me? You must know what I'm talking about, but you have to keep this just between us two for now," chats Geoff excitedly.

"You really are an idiot, Geoff," says Rose, drinking the last drop of her wine and ready to leave the pub in an instant.

"I'm only going to take a few jars of the stuff. That's all I'll need. Just a few jars of it, that's all I'm saying," says Geoff, taking their glasses up towards the bar to be refilled. Rose sighs. She has just given him up as completely hopeless, just this minute. There seems to be no hope for him anymore, she ponders to herself.

She can see Geoff already at the bar getting refills and she thinks this will be a good time for her to leave him to his own devices, for good, when she hears the throbbing engine of Roger's red Porsche turn the corner, then drive into the pub car park and park just outside the window where they sit.

Rose sits down immediately and starts to panic. She can't let Roger find them having a drink together. Geoff soon returns with their drink refills and can tell Rose looks panicked. He then notices Roger's Porsche through the window ahead of him.

Though the window he watches Roger fumble around in his driver's seat, just about ready to get out and he knows this will look bad for Rose, as well as him, if he finds them in here together.

Outside in the car park, Roger slams his car door closed, then strides towards the door of the pub with his face red with anger. He throws open the door to find Rose sitting all alone at the table ahead of him.

"Okay, Rose, where have you hidden him?" fumes Roger. Roger scans the pub for signs of Geoff but he can't see him.

"Sit down, Roger. Have a drink. I'll pay," says Rose nervously fumbling around in her handbag for some cash.

Roger's face reddens even more when he can't find Geoff in the pub. He looks out of the window at his car. "I saw him outside the school. I've had enough, Rose. You're putting our relationship in jeopardy every time you have anything to do with him from now on. Have you got that?" says Roger angrily.

Rose nods nervously, agreeing with him. She knows he knows Geoff has been here and she doesn't know what else to say so she begins to cry.

"It was just a drink. He's going to turn things around. He's promised he will do," says Rose, holding onto Roger's arm.

"I know somewhere deep down you're trying to help him; trying to help a fellow teacher in their hour of need and all that but every time you try to help him from now on, it will mean we're moving one step closer to the end of our relationship. I'm sure you understand that. Geoff's none of our business anymore," says Roger, releasing Rose's arm from his.

Outside in the car park, Geoff crouches by the side of Roger's Porsche, unseen. He can hear their heated discussion through the door of the pub not far away.

Geoff goes to the furthest tyre of Roger's car, then begins to release the air out of it as he listens to Roger's tirade inside the pub. As he does so, Roger's angry face soon appears at the window. Has he seen him? Geoff crouches even lower.

Inside the pub, Roger slowly calms a little when he finds no evidence of Geoff still being there. "Well, I've scared him away it seems, good thing too. It's in your best interests to leave Geoff alone. To leave him be," says Roger, straightening himself up in his oversized suit and feeling pleased with himself that he's got the presence to scare away the competition.

"But what about Geoff's best interests?" replies Rose looking around the pub, wondering where Geoff has got to.

Roger's in no mood to sit down and have a drink with Rose. He storms out of the pub quite satisfied that Geoff has been frightened away. He quickly scans the busy car park for signs of the drunken monster but he can't see him, so he jumps back towards his sports car.

Geoff is taken unawares by Roger's speedy exit from the pub. He thought he would have more time. As he crouches he can sense Roger on the other side of the Porsche, scanning the car park. Geoff can crouch no longer. He scrambles away from Roger's car just before Roger storms towards the driver's side to beep his key fob and open the Porsche door.

Geoff scampers away from Roger's car towards his own battered old car on the other side of the car park.

He slips inside it, then quietly and slowly closes his car door, keeping his head as low as he can. He hopes that Roger has not seen his old car in the car park.

Roger's about to climb into his car when he spots Geoff's battered old vehicle on the other side of the car park. He stares at Geoff's car for a while but once he's satisfied there's no one inside it, he gets into his Porsche and slams the door closed.

He starts the engine. It throbs, instantly causing several of the people sitting outside having a drink to grab their glasses and retreat towards the back of the pub garden, in fear of the loud throbbing noise.

Roger revs the engine even louder, because he is that angry and he can see the effect it has on some of the locals. It's not long before the pub landlord appears at the door to find out what the commotion is all about.

The landlord then watches Roger's Porsche wheel spin towards the entrance of the pub, leaving him to feel relieved that this troublemaker is getting off his premises. He is relieved, that is, until he finds Roger's sports car pulling up at the pub entrance with a loud skid. Something's wrong with Roger's pride and joy.

Roger jumps out, then inspects the two flat tyres on one side of his car. Roger fumes as he shakes his fists at Geoff's empty, battered old car parked further back in the car park.

Several of those drinking outside burst into chuckles that now make Roger's fuming face a maroon colour. Roger kicks one of the flat tyres in frustration. "Aghhh," cries Roger.

He turns to find the spectators outside the pub in no mood to stop chuckling, so Roger slopes back inside his car then drives his Porsche, even with the two flat tyres, out of the pub car park.

As all this is going on, Geoff remains slouched in his car hoping that Roger has not seen him or walk over to his car to inflict some kind of revenge damage.

So when the passenger door to Geoff's battered old car does open in the car park, several moments later, he feels as scared as he felt when Heckton pinned him against the side of the corridor wall some weeks before.

Geoff ducks his head even lower, expecting to see Roger's irate face peer towards him, but when the much-kinder face of Rose appears and she then jumps into the passenger seat next to him, he lets out a deep sigh of relief.

"Roger gets so possessive. It makes me so angry," says Rose, closing the car door once she's made herself more comfortable.

Chapter 6

Later that evening, Geoff drives his car along the gravel drive towards Appleby's lighted farmhouse with Rose sitting next to him. "Where are you taking me?" asks Rose.

"I told you earlier at the Bricklayers Arms – I need your help. What's the time?" asks Geoff, parking his car outside the kitchen of the farmhouse.

"Nine thirty," replies Rose, suddenly getting a sense of where Geoff has driven her to. "You've kept this quiet since we were at the pub at lunch time."

"I wasn't sure what Roger would do about his tyres," replies Geoff.

"He hasn't done anything about it. He pumped his tyres up at the garage and went back to school. He seemed okay at the end of the day," says Rose.

"That's what frightens me. What's he got up his sleeve, I wonder," replies Geoff.

"I am sure he hasn't got anything up his sleeve. All he needs to do is to wait for you to show what you've got up your sleeve and then he'll pounce. And he hasn't needed to wait for long, judging by where you have just driven us to," says Rose.

"Appleby will be in 'The Farmer's Chair,' completely sozzled by now, hopefully," replies Geoff, "but we must be quick," he adds.

"This isn't Russell Appleby's place, is it? Please tell me this isn't his farmhouse and you're not going to break into it and steal some silly jars of honey? Please tell me you're not," asks Rose anxiously.

"There's no sign of his four-by-four and I'm not going to break into his farmhouse," replies Geoff, opening his car door.

"Then where are you going? What are you going to do here while he's out?" asks Rose.

"I told you – Appleby keeps his honey in the barn nearby. I'm sure of it. You stay here. Start the car if you hear anything," says Geoff, closing his car door quietly.

"Geoff! You can't leave me here!" says Rose into the darkness that has already swallowed Geoff up.

Geoff scampers over the gravel driveway, then creeps around the side of the farmhouse until he can see the large barn that stands just behind the farmhouse kitchen.

He peeks through the farmhouse kitchen window just to make sure no one is there, then scampers over to the large barn door ahead of him. Geoff tries the door handle of the small door built inside the larger barn door. It opens easily and quietly.

Geoff creeps inside the dark barn. He lights over the barn with flashes from his torch until he finds what he's looking for. He then moves through the darkness towards a large fridge that's almost hidden in the furthest corner of the barn.

He can hear a deep humming coming from somewhere and this brings him to a stop for a moment. He flashes over the barn with his torch but he can't see any bees, so he scampers on over to the fridge and opens its door.

Geoff's eyes widen with amazement at the golden glare of twenty or thirty jars of honey illuminated by the light of the fridge. They glisten like jars of treasure and Geoff's tempted to stuff them all into his old, brown overcoat.

"Oh, honey, honey, honey..." says Geoff excitedly.

He lights over the barn behind him with his torch to check he's still on his own, then stuffs about twelve jars full of the honey into his overcoat. He then slams the fridge door closed and dashes through the darkness towards the open barn door.

He's almost reached the small barn door when he hears the unmistakable click of a rifle from somewhere in the darkness ahead. It brings Geoff to a skidding halt. He still can't see anything because he's turned his torch off and he's tempted to make a run for the barn door anyway, but something menacing and purposeful about the heavy click makes Geoff stand perfectly still where he is and switch his torch on to search for a foe hidden in the darkness.

His torch light freezes when it locks onto what Geoff has been dreading. Russell Appleby squints under the glare of Geoff's torch light as he points his loaded rifle straight at him.

"I couldn't resist, Russ," pleads Geoff.

Geoff can tell by Appleby's eyes that he's half-cut. "Empty your pockets then get out of here before I blast you away," says Appleby, rather too calmly.

"Do you really think that anyone has ever jumped through a field the way I jumped through those fields last night? You've got something special here and we need to find out what makes it so," replies Geoff, already approaching Appleby with his hands held out open in front of him.

"I thought I could trust you. That you could help me. You looked like you needed a break when I first saw you," says Appleby.

"Look, Russ, what you've got here – well, I don't really know what you've got here, but I can help you. It is gold, pure gold," replies Geoff.

"My finger's on the trigger!" shouts Appleby, raising his rifle again to point it straight at him when he senses Geoff move from his spot.

Geoff's scared. He's fairly sure Appleby will shoot him if he tries to escape, so he puts his hands up and moves sideways towards the open barn door.

"Remove all the jars of honey from your coat and put them on the ground," says Appleby, moving towards him with his rifle still pointed.

Geoff has no choice. The open barn door remains tantalisingly close but then he looks to the rifle pointed straight at him, so he slowly removes one jar of the honey from his overcoat and puts it onto the ground in front of him.

Then he slowly takes out another jar and puts it onto the ground too. It has the desired effect. Appleby relaxes just enough and his attention is broken just long enough for Geoff to jump out of the open barn door and disappear into the darkness with the remaining jars of honey before the drunken Appleby knows what's happening.

Geoff does not look back. He sprints away through the darkness as two loud gunshots ring out loudly from inside the barn. Two gunshots blast through the wooden barn door behind him. then whistle through the air over Geoff's head. Geoff ducks, then sprints on past the farmhouse kitchen and around the corner towards his car.

He quickly opens his car door then jumps inside, yelping with excitement. "I have the merchandise, Rose."

Rose has already got the car engine running so Geoff wheel-spins his car backwards along the gravel driveway, then out of the farm and into the darkness of the night.

The next morning, Max Heckton strides along the school corridor looking aggressive and mean and feeling exactly the same way, so when he sees the long black-caped headmaster, Anthony Bright, walk around the corner ahead of him, his strides turn into a run until he catches up with him.

"I've been hearing more things about Geoff Wade, headmaster," says Heckton, menacingly.

"Have you now?" replies the headmaster.

"From what I understand, he's been upsetting some of the teachers even though he's still on a suspension," says Heckton, grinning and baring his teeth at the same time.

"I have heard nothing and how can Geoff be upsetting teachers if he isn't even here?" replies the headmaster.

"Exactly, sir. That's what's troubling me," says Heckton.

"I think what I can deduce, from the little you have told me about it, is that this isn't any of your business, Max," replies Bright.

"It may turn out to be our business," says Heckton.

"What do you mean by that?" replies Bright.

"He's up to something. Geoff's always up to something, inside or outside school," says Heckton.

"So these accusations you are making are really just a hunch of yours?" replies Bright.

"Do you want me to quieten him so that he doesn't cause this school any more problems?" says Heckton frustratingly, suddenly turning very angry and sinister looking.

"What did you say, Max?" replies Bright questioningly but seemingly very used to Heckton's sudden angry bouts of trouble making.

"Do you want me to make sure that he never gets up to any more funny business in the future?" says Heckton clearly, whilst baring his upper right teeth.

"I'm not sure what you mean, Max. I'll pretend I didn't hear that," says Bright, trying to walk swiftly away from Heckton without success.

"What I want to hear is that you're not reviewing his suspension any time soon, are you?" asks Heckton.

"What business is it of yours?" replies the headmaster. "His suspension will be reviewed when it is due to be reviewed. I've told you about this before, Max: if I need your help I'll ask for it. Concentrate on your own teaching. I hear Year Nine aren't where they should be in Geography," replies the headmaster, as he steps up his pace to finally escape from Heckton in the crowded corridor.

Heckton fumes as he watches the headmaster sweep away around the corner ahead of him. Heckton hates not getting his way. His attention is soon grabbed by Rose walking towards him. Rose smiles at him as best she can, only for Heckton to return an aggressive and mean stare back. Rose sighs deeply and walks on past him without talking to him.

Rose saunters into the staffroom moments after her unpleasant but quiet exchange with Heckton. The room throngs with stressed-looking teachers and it takes her a while to find a chair to sit down on. She eventually finds a seat next to Valerie Coott, another fellow English teacher.

After a brief exchange between Rose and Valerie, headmaster, Anthony Bright, strides commandingly into the staffroom wearing his long, black gown. The stressed-looking teachers around him immediately go quiet and wait hopefully for some words of wisdom from their leader to ease their predicaments, whatever they may be.

Bright ignores them all this morning and takes his seat on a raised platform at one end of the staffroom. He shuffles a few papers he holds in his hands before rising and placing the papers on the lectern in front of him. He looks as stressed as the other teachers sitting around him.

"Let's start with some good news, shall we? As you know, Mr Wade has been on suspension for the past few weeks."

"Boo. . ." cries Rose from the back of the room.

"However, after speaking with one of my colleagues this morning, I have decided that we should welcome him back as soon as he is able to return," continues the headmaster, giving Max Heckton a stern stare that leaves Heckton with his mouth dropped open in disbelief as he stands cross-armed next to the staffroom door. Heckton then bares his angry yellow teeth towards Bright, which makes the headmaster smile and feel better about his morning already.

"Here, here!" cries Rose, quite surprised by the headmaster's U-turn. There's a low mumbling and grumbling from the other teachers in the room, most of whom would prefer not to see Geoff return to the school, which is the reason why Bright then gives Rose a big smile to acknowledge her expressed sentiments.

The headmaster feels pleased with his sudden change of heart over Geoff and it fills him with even more confidence for the day ahead.

"And I have more welcome news; this time for our overworked and overstretched woodwork department. Mr Philpott's social mobility scooter has at last been found and returned to the school after spending several days under a bridge on the other side of town. Mr Philpott will be returning to the school this Friday. So that means two of our hard-working teachers will be returning to the school by the beginning of next week," says Bright triumphantly.

"Hoorah!" cry out some of the teachers sarcastically, while others mumble and grumble in disagreement.

"Now, back to some less pleasant news: the parent-teacher evening has been rearranged for this Thursday," states Bright.

"You must be joking!" cries out Valerie Coott.

"I wish I were, Valerie, but we can't hold off the parent-teacher evening forever. Many parents are getting restless and asking questions as to why it has been delayed for so long," replies Bright, expecting a backlash from his overworked staff but not getting one. "I'll be asking for volunteers to sign up this afternoon," he adds, finishing the morning debriefing hastily but not before noticing the look Rose gives him as he quickly gathers up his papers from the lectern, ready to stride back out of the staffroom.

Bright seems distracted and unable to stop to talk to the other teachers today and he disappears out of the staffroom saying no more, leaving many of the teachers feeling frustrated that they could not get his attention. Rose watches her headmaster stride out of the staffroom from the sidelines. She then lets out a long sigh.

At around lunchtime, later that day, Geoff's battered old car speeds along a winding country lane. His unwashed, long and unkempt hair blows in the wind through the open window. Geoff's mobile phone rings on the seat next to him. He tries to pick it up but accidentally swipes it off the seat, making it fall down out of sight. The phone continues to ring as Geoff looks at his bloodshot eyes in the mirror.

He turns into the school road and parks his car outside the school. It's not long before he sees Rose run towards his car with a wide smile across her face. She opens Geoff's passenger car door and excitedly jumps into the passenger seat. Geoff wonders what he has done to make her smile like this.

"You see, I told you the headmaster was on your side," says Rose breathlessly.

Geoff wonders what she is talking about and when he notices Roger give him a stern stare over the roof of his Porsche, in the school car park not far away from him, he crunches through his gears to drive his car as far away from the school as possible.

"He ain't on my side, sister," replies Geoff finally.

"Just accept some good news gracefully for once, will you," says Rose.

"What good news?" replies Geoff, now looking at her.

"Didn't you look at your phone?" asks Rose.

"No, it's lodged under your seat somewhere," he replies.

"The headmaster wants you back at the school as soon as possible," says Rose.

"You think that's good news, going back to that place?" replies Geoff feeling miserable.

"Of course it is. Look at the state of you. You don't know what you're doing when you're not teaching," replies Rose, making Geoff accelerate his car away, feeling upset that Rose is right yet again.

Rose sighs. "Why are you so difficult, all of the time?" she asks.

"I'm not difficult, Rose. It's just you: you're so irritating. You don't know anyone interested in buying some honey, do you?" replies Geoff.

"You've still got that stuff?" asks Rose.

"Of course. It's still in the boot. I don't know what to do with it. I'm scared of trying any more of it," says Geoff.

"Get rid of it, that's what you should do with it. Appleby's probably already reported it stolen and reported you, too," replies Rose, slapping her head completely forgetting about last night's little incident.

"I doubt it," says Geoff.

"You doubt what?" asks Rose looking at him.

"No one's going to be searching for a few jars of honey, are they?" says Geoff.

"You broke into his barn last night. Besides, I thought you would have arranged a sale of the stuff before you stole it," replies Rose.

"So, you're an expert on stolen goods now?" says Geoff.

Rose sighs deeply. "Look at you, Geoff: you smell. Go and take a bath or something and leave me out of your problems," replies Rose, now quite disgusted with Geoff's behaviour and demeanour.

"Stop being so. . ." says Geoff unable to find the right word.

"Sensible? Grown up?" replies Rose.

"Righteous. You're such a righteous babe, all the time," says Geoff.

"Too right I am. It keeps me in shape and it keeps me happy and content. Do you know what that means? To be happy and content?" replies Rose.

Geoff feels ill and starts to grumble under his breath, while Rose looks around the countryside they drive through, not quite sure where they are.

"But it is good news about you coming back to the school," says Rose changing tack.

"Did you have a word with the headmaster?" asks Geoff.

"No – that's what's so good about it. I thought the less I said to him about you, the better," replies Rose. "Where are we going, though? I thought we were going out for lunch?" adds Rose.

"Can't," replies Geoff.

"Why can't we?" asks Rose.

"Appleby will have his henchman out looking for me," replies Geoff.

"How old are you, Geoff? Appleby hasn't got any henchman. If you've still got that honey, just dump it somewhere or better still, take the jars back to his farm," says Rose with a sigh.

"Too late for that now: he'll be after me," replies Geoff.

"If you've still got that honey in the boot, find a field right now and we'll get rid of it," says Rose, looking at the back seat to make sure it isn't there. "You're afraid of him, aren't you?" she says.

"I'm not taking any chances," says Geoff. "He did shoot at me last night."

"That was in the heat of the moment. He was probably drunk, too. Appleby's a farmer – he's not like that, is he? Revengeful?" asks Rose.

"I don't know for sure. He could well be like that. Especially with his precious honey," replies Geoff.

Rose sighs. She considers their predicament. "Geoff, what are you like? You're constantly on the move – changing, physically, mentally and emotionally. I just can't get hold of you anymore. Just try and slow down a bit, will you?"

"Is that why you left me?" asks Geoff. "I'm too fast for you?"

"Roger's so steady and reliable. I know where I am with him. It makes me happy. Why can't you be more like him? Why can't you be more. . . be more boring," says Rose. "Now, slow down."

"I'm not sure what you mean by slow down," says Geoff honestly. "I've been on suspension for weeks. I can't get any slower than that, can I?"

"No, I mean, literally – slow down a bit, right now! There's a car turning onto our road right in front of us!" cries Rose, in panic, as an SUV turns out of a T-junction just in front of them.

Geoff grabs hard on the steering wheel, then drives his car into the side of the road to try and avoid the SUV heading straight for them, but it is too late. The large SUV crashes into the rear of Geoff's car, pushing it up the muddy bank at the side of the road.

Geoff and Rose slump back into their seats, quite shaken but grateful that their seat belts held.

"Are you all right?" asks Geoff.

"Just about," replies Rose.

Geoff's car slides back down the side of the muddy bank and back onto the road. Geoff looks into his mirror to find the large SUV still standing behind them. He expects to see the driver get out of his car any minute to check that they are okay, but it doesn't take long for Geoff to realise that the SUV that has just crashed into them belongs to the one person that he is most anxious to avoid: Russell Appleby.

Geoff can hear the SUV's accelerator revving its engine behind them and he genuinely fears for their safety. His fears are heightened when he focuses on the driver of the SUV in his mirror.

Russell Appleby stares towards him with his teeth gritted and his hands gripping firmly on the steering wheel in anger. Geoff immediately and fortunately manages to start his car again. He accelerates quickly away along the country lane as fast as he can, while Rose sits next to him, almost rigid with fear, and holding tightly onto the handrail above her door.

Geoff speeds along the country lane with only one thing on his mind: to get as far away from Russell Appleby as he possibly can.

"Geoff, slow down! For goodness sake, slow down!" cries Rose still gripping hold of the handrail.

Geoff does not slow down because Appleby's SUV chases hard after them, until it is close enough for it to bump into the back of Geoff's car. Their car jerks forward from the bump, making Rose turn towards Geoff.

"It's Appleby, isn't it?" asks Rose, already knowing the answer.

"It's a very angry-looking Appleby, too. He can't know where I live, can he? He must have seen my car," says Geoff as they both feel the SUV bump into the back of their car again.

"For God's sake, Geoff – give Appleby back his honey!" cries Rose desperately.

Geoff soon notices a turning into a field close on their left-hand side. He skids, then turns the steering wheel sharply, taking their car into the field. He then accelerates his car through the field along a readymade track in the earth, hoping that Appleby has not reacted quickly enough and driven straight past the turning.

Geoff's right. Appleby's SUV skids to a halt on the country lane but he's reacted too slowly. His SUV skids on past the entrance to the field. Appleby fumes then reverses angrily backwards until he can wheelspin his SUV into the field, in pursuit.

Geoff looks excitedly in his mirror, now enjoying the thrill of the chase, even though he's the one being chased. Rose looks to him knowingly and worryingly.

"That guy's nuts," says Geoff, as Appleby's SUV soon closes quickly on them along the track in the field.

"Stop the car! Stop the car, right now!" cries Rose anxiously. But Geoff does not stop because he can see in his mirror that Appleby's in no mood to negotiate.

Appleby's SUV chases Geoff's battered old car through the fields under a cloudless, sunny sky with Geoff, having no idea as to where they are or where they're heading.

Geoff and Rose shake up and down inside the battered old car as they ride over the rough ground with Appleby's SUV constantly crashing into the back of them.

"Shoot his tyres, Rose. Slow him down a bit," says Geoff, looking towards a terrified-looking Rose, who still has both hands gripped onto the hand rail above her door.

"I'm going to faint!" says Rose, closing her eyes and going very white.

Geoff can finally see a turning out of the field. He skids his car off the dried tractor-made tracks in the earth, then heads over even rougher terrain towards a gap between the hedges. Appleby's SUV skids to a halt behind him, then changes tack in pursuit.

Unluckily for Geoff, the gap in the hedges turns out not to be a turning back onto the road but a turning into another field. Geoff has no option but to drive onwards through one field after another, until his battered old car looks even more battered and bruised than before and the engine sounds even worse than it has ever sounded.

Geoff fears that his car may conk out at any minute, so he's relieved to see a turning ahead out of the field where he can actually see the winding country lane lead onwards from it. He skids out of the field and turns his steering wheel sharply to get the car back onto the tarmac of the country lane.

He looks in his mirror to find the lane behind him still empty for a moment and wonders if Appleby's car has conked out instead. He relaxes slightly but as he does so he fails to notice a bridge that traverses a fast-flowing river approach them quickly.

"Geoff! The bridge!" cries out Rose, knowing Geoff has not seen it.

Geoff quickly focuses back onto the road in front of him but it's too late. He tries to veer the car very sharply onto the bridge but he can't. The car rides up the bank just before the bridge, crashes through some thin fencing by the side of it, then down the steep bank until their car flies into the middle of the fast-flowing and deep river.

"Aghh!" cries Rose, as the car sinks quickly around her. Geoff quickly winds down his window before the car's completely submerged, so that as the car sinks towards the bottom of the deep river, Geoff heroically pulls Rose out of the passenger seat, then hauls her through the open window where the water rushes in.

Once they are both clear of the car, they both swim towards the surface then paddle over towards the bank of the river. Geoff hauls Rose towards the river bank until they can both feel the wet grass.

Geoff finally raises his head out of the water to try and haul himself onto the bank but instead of finding the river bank, he finds a hand reaching down towards him. Geoff grabs at the hand, which then pulls him completely out of the river.

He looks up into the face of Russell Appleby. Appleby then helps Rose onto the river bank, where she lies breathing heavily but still in shock. No one says anything for a moment, leaving Geoff to look back towards the river where his car has now sunk completely below the surface.

Chapter 7

Max Heckton stands at the front of the class staring angrily at his pupils, while he waits for someone to answer his question. The pupils bow their heads when he looks straight at them, as he tries to prise out an answer.

In the corner of the classroom he notices Ernest Thompson look out of the window towards the river that runs just outside.

"I'm still waiting for an answer, anyone? Thompson – look this way, please," says Heckton, quite forcefully.

Thompson lifts himself out of a daydream when he hears his name mentioned and looks towards the diagram drawn on the whiteboard behind the teacher, but still looks clueless.

"Surely, you must know the answer, Ernest?" asks Heckton, ever hopefully.

"Yes, sir," replies Thompson.

"Yes, sir – what, sir?" asks Heckton again, feeling quite exasperated.

"What, sir?" replies Thompson.

"What does this diagram on the board demonstrate?" asks Heckton, now fuming.

Heckton is forced to look to his other pupils for an answer, even though Thompson has now upset Heckton for the rest of the lesson and it doesn't escape his notice that Thompson returns to looking out of the window. Heckton fumes when he sees this and returns to stare at the disobedient Thompson while his face turns crimson.

"Thompson!" shouts Heckton angrily.

"I've been looking at the formation of the ox-bow lake on the river outside, sir," replies Thompson, just in time before Heckton throws a book at him.

Heckton turns and writes, 'Ox-Bow Lake' above the diagram on the board behind him.

"Detention for you, Thompson, if you look out of that window one more time," he says, baring his angry teeth.

Thompson straightens up in his chair to focus completely on the diagram on the board at the front of the classroom behind Heckton. Heckton keeps his eyes on him, just as Thompson quickly glances out of the window, even though he keeps his head strictly pointing forwards towards Heckton.

"Detention, Thompson," says Heckton.

"Oh, sir, I had something in my eye," replies Thompson.

There's a heavy knocking on the classroom door that forces Heckton's attention away from the disobedient Thompson. Headmaster Bright opens the door then pokes his head inside the classroom.

"Can I have a quick word, Max?" says Bright, smiling at the pupils.

Heckton goes to meet him at the door. "Have you seen, Miss Daniels?" asks Bright.

"Not since early this morning," replies Heckton.

"No one has seen her since lunchtime. She has a class now," says Bright. "Why come to me? Why would I know where she is? Try Geoff Wade," replies Heckton.

"I've asked Roger Little and he hasn't seen her since coffee time. I'm a little concerned: it's not like her," says the headmaster, now convinced that Heckton is right about Rose's whereabouts. "Thank you, Max," he adds, as he closes the door.

Bright strides away from the classroom back along the corridor with heavy footsteps while listening to Heckton's loud and forceful voice in the classroom behind him.

"Right – detention, Sarah Jordan," fumes Heckton.

"Oh, sir," replies Jordan miserably, just as the headmaster's billowing gown disappears around the corner of the corridor.

The moon shines brightly over the old stone bridge that crosses the fast-flowing and deep river that runs through Honibridge. There is the sound of two large splashes into the river at the base of the bridge, where it meets with the water that breaks the silence of the night.

Two wet-suited figures with oxygen tanks on their backs and waterproof torches in their hands swim down through the river towards the car that lies below them on the bottom of the riverbed.

Despite the water flowing quickly on the surface, the water is very clear the deeper they dive, so that they can see the car quite clearly below them as they approach. The boot of the car has opened as it crashed into the river, so the two approaching torches shine clearly over the glistening jars of honey in the boot of Geoff's battered old car.

The two wet-suited figures reach the car quickly and waste no time in loading the jars of honey into a holdall. They then swim back towards the surface of the river.

The two figures soon reach the surface where they pull their oxygen mouthpieces out. "We've got all of them and they're all still in one piece?" asks Appleby anxiously from the middle of the river.

"Yep," replies Geoff succinctly and with relief as he swims towards the side of the river holding the holdall. Appleby reaches the riverbank first.

He helps Geoff out of the river, then grabs the holdall full of the intact jars of honey from him quite forcefully.

"I'm afraid my car's a write-off though," says Geoff to deaf ears as he looks back towards the river, while Appleby makes his way towards his SUV without saying anything else.

Appleby's SUV pulls up on the gravel driveway of his farmhouse some short time afterwards. Appleby then jumps out and carries the holdall into the kitchen still without saying anything to Geoff or Rose.

"He never said anything to us all the way here," says Rose to Geoff.

Geoff is not sure whether they should have anything more to do with Appleby from now on. He's returned the honey intact to him, so he thinks it may be better just to walk away and forget he ever got involved with the matter. Appleby seems to have forgiven him for stealing it, he thinks.

Rose remains quiet on the back seat, probably thinking about the same thing as Geoff. They look to each other. It would make more sense for them to just leave Appleby well alone from now on, they both think silently to themselves.

Inside the farmhouse kitchen, Appleby places the full holdall of honey onto the kitchen table, then removes some of his wetsuit. It's quite a surprise to him that Geoff and Rose waddle into his kitchen shortly afterwards. Appleby immediately throws a towel towards Geoff to dry himself down.

"All of this stays between the three of us, you got that?" says Appleby finally.

"But what about the car?" asks Rose.

"Yeah, we got it," replies Geoff speaking for the both of them.

"The fridge in the barn contains the last of my special honey. If we lose that, then maybe we'll never be able to replicate it. Who knows when the bees will stop being so obliging with this special honey they're making at the moment?" says Appleby, slipping out of his wetsuit while Rose ogles him. "We have to keep these jars of honey a secret for now, for all our sakes," he adds, tasting some of the honey from one of the jars they have just rescued from the deep.

"Yes – okay, Russell. We understand," says Rose, taking a seat at the kitchen table while Appleby and Geoff get dressed.

"I'm not sure that you do, completely, because you've only seen some of what this honey is capable of. I have since discovered it has some other properties," says Appleby, taking two jars of honey out of his kitchen fridge. He opens one of them, then passes it to Geoff.

"The honey in the barn that you stole and have already tried is almost six-months old. These two jars here, I've been working on and guess what? I've managed to synthesise the honey to create something even more potent," says Appleby, widening his eyes with excitement.

"So it's not just for high-jumpers anymore?" asks Geoff.

"Exactly! Well, it's for high-jumpers, too," says Appleby excitedly.

He hands one of the special jars of honey to Rose and the other one to Geoff. Rose eyes the jar with suspicion.

"You mean this stuff is even more dangerous than the jars you've already synthesised?" she asks.

"Not dangerous!" replies Appleby.

But Rose is not convinced. "I think we should go, Geoff," she says sensibly.

"You can't go now! I've let you both into this secret and I expect some kind of loyalty from both of you," says Appleby.

"I think Rose is right. We will stay quiet on the whole matter but we should have no further dealings with you," replies Geoff.

"But you must! You must try this new synthesised honey! You simply must!" says Appleby.

"You want us to try it now?" asks Rose.

"No, no – take it home with you. Just one word of warning: don't, under any circumstances, take some of it just after you've been exercising. Try it when you're marking some homework or something. Yes – try it then: that would be an ideal time," says Appleby, wide-eyed.

Rose pushes her jar of honey back towards Appleby. "I'm not trying any of it. Why shouldn't we take it after we've just been exercising? Sounds all very suspicious. You really mean you want to use us two as your guinea pigs?" she asks.

"I've tried it on myself. I'm the original guinea pig," retorts Appleby.

Geoff feels guilty about stealing the other jars of honey in the first place, so he feels he can't just turn his back on Appleby now.

"I'll try it, Russ," he pipes up.

"Good, good. I thought you might," replies Appleby.

Rose does not know what to do. She can't afford to upset Appleby too much because he may get Geoff into trouble. "I'm still not trying any of it until I know what it'll do. I'll keep all this a secret between us three, for Geoff's sake, but I am not trying any of it myself – you got that?" says Rose, getting up from the table feeling uncomfortable.

Now it's Geoff's turn to feel uncomfortable. He has no idea where all of this will lead, so he decides to refuse the honey, too, even though he knows Appleby could get him into trouble for breaking into his barn.

"You know, Rose is right. I've just got my job back so I can't risk anything at the moment. I've got to keep as low a profile as I can," says Geoff to an impressed-looking Rose but to an upset-looking Appleby.

Geoff reluctantly slides his jar of the synthesised honey back towards Appleby and then gets up to leave, as well. They both walk towards the kitchen door.

"We'll keep it a secret, Russ, don't you worry about that," he says. "But you really should find someone who knows something more about all of this synthesised honey and talk to them about it," adds Geoff as he opens the door.

"But what use are you two if you don't help me? I need test subjects. I need people who can test this stuff out for me before I can take it to anyone else. I need to make sure it works," replies Appleby looking concerned.

Geoff and Rose walk slowly out of the door, just as Appleby says what they have both been dreading. "What if I were to tell someone at your school that you broke into my barn last night?" adds Appleby, feeling desperate. Geoff is forced to turn back towards him.

"You wouldn't tell anyone at our school," says Geoff.

"Why wouldn't I?" adds Appleby.

"Because we would then explain to them exactly what you've got in your barn. Then someone would be along the next day to take a look at all of your precious honey," replies Geoff.

Appleby takes a seat looking defeated and sad.

"You're a nasty piece of work, Appleby. Did you know that?" says Rose angrily. "You're trying to get us into trouble and that's the last thing Geoff needs right now."

"I just want to know what we have here in these little jars. I've tried it. I need more proof. Don't you want to know, too? Think of the financial rewards, Geoff. You've already seen what the original honey can do," says Appleby, moving the two jars of synthesised honey back towards him.

Geoff re-enters the kitchen, despite Rose trying to hold him back outside. He grabs one jar of the honey then puts it into his jacket pocket. He then walks back out of the kitchen door without saying another word.

Several days later, Geoff walks briskly towards his classroom on the first day back after his suspension. His hair is washed and combed and he wears a brand new shirt given to him by Rose. He feels good, refreshed and free from a hangover, so he enters the classroom full of life and vigour.

His Year Eleven students sit attentively and quietly at their desks in front of him, when he enters the classroom. He confidently unpacks his backpack full of books onto the desk at the front of the room because he's prepared for today's lesson and he knows exactly what he's going to teach them.

But something makes him stop in his tracks. There's something lying at the bottom of his backpack, which he can't take his eyes off for a moment. He can't hear the quiet chatter of the pupils in front of him because his mind is focused on the glistening jar of honey lying at the bottom of his bag, which he had quite forgotten about until now.

"Nice to see you back, sir," says Ernest Thompson, trying to get his attention.

"Yeah, did you enjoy your holiday? At the pub!" says Sarah Jordan, making all of the pupils laugh.

Geoff only half hears them and he's in such a good mood, anyway, that he says nothing in reply. Yet the jar of honey somehow beckons to him from the bottom of his backpack and despite all the good advice that Rose has given him over the past few days, he's unable to resist the lure of the glistening jar. He springs into action.

"I'll be back in just a minute, class," says Geoff, leaving his books on the desk and carrying his mostly empty backpack back out of the classroom with him.

Sarah Jordan is slightly taken aback by his actions and wonders if she has upset Mr. Wade already. The class go quiet, too, when he leaves the room, all thinking the same thing as Sarah Jordan.

Geoff returns to the classroom a short while later, carrying a jug full of water and two dozen beakers on a tray. Each beaker contains some concentrated blackcurrant juice with some of Appleby's honey mixed in with it.

"A little celebration on my return, Year Eleven," says Geoff, holding out one of the beakers that he has just filled with water from the jug.

All the pupils dash to the front of the class to get their drink, while Geoff fills each beaker with water. "Take your time. There's a drink for each of you and help yourself to a biscuit, too," says Geoff, opening a packet of custard cream biscuits.

"What is this – blackcurrant?" asks Thompson.

"I'm surprised it's not something stronger, sir, coming from you," says Ben Andrews.

"Less of the cheek, Andrews," replies Geoff, watching them all drink the honeyed blackcurrant juice with great gusto, as well as seeing them fillet the packet of biscuits almost as soon as it is opened.

"Right – if you've all had a celebratory drink and biscuit, return to your desks and we'll crack on with the lesson," says Geoff packing away the empty beakers.

Geoff gets straight to work and draws some trigonometry diagrams on the board in front of him, while his pupils tap away on their calculators to work out the answers.

"Now, Lomax, what answer do you have for the first question?" asks Geoff.

"Seventy-nine degrees?" replies Lomax, holding up his calculator at the back of the classroom for Geoff to see.

"And you, Andrews?" asks Geoff.

"Seventy-nine degrees," replies Andrews, who is slightly surprised he has the same answer as Lomax.

"And Ernest Thompson?" asks Geoff.

"Is the answer seventy-nine degrees, sir?" asks Ernest Thompson, looking at his calculator, disbelieving his eyes that he has calculated the same answer as the others.

"That is correct. Did we all get seventy-nine degrees?" asks Geoff with a smile on his face, half expecting them to all have the correct answer, even before they tell him.

"You should all give yourselves a round of applause. You're all correct for perhaps the first time in this class. Well done," says Geoff as a few of his students give themselves a half-hearted clap. "Now, looking at this more difficult question I have just drawn on the board?" says Geoff.

"Twenty-six degrees, sir," says Thompson, almost immediately.

"Slow down – you'll need your calculator, Ernest, to work out the answer," says Geoff tapping away at his calculator. He calculates the answer to be twenty-six degrees.

"A lucky guess, Thompson?" asks Geoff.

"I worked it out in my head," says Thompson surprisingly.

"Yeah, I made it twenty-six degrees, too. I used my calculator though," pipes up Sarah Jordan.

"It was no guesswork, sir. That is the correct answer. You're such a good teacher, sir – that's why," replies Thompson with a smile.

Geoff slumps into his seat behind his desk. He and Rose had half expected this to be the outcome of the jars of honey that Appleby had given them but he hadn't expected the honey to have worked quite as well as this. He leans back in his chair with a nervous smile on his face.

Chapter 8

Marjorie Philpott brings a pot of tea into the front room of her small but well cared-for house located very near to the centre of Honibridge. Her husband, Mitchell Philpott, looks at her from across the breakfast table.

"Pass the marmalade, dear," says Mitchell, quite grumpily.

"Pass the marmalade, please," corrects Marjorie, before passing him the jar of marmalade.

Mitchell grabs the jar from her too quickly, spilling the contents over their deep red, patterned carpet.

"Oh, Mitchell," says Marjorie, immediately getting to her knees to clear up the mess, while Mitchell stands on his two crutches as if to say he certainly can't clear it up for her.

"You know, perhaps it may be best for you not to go in today. You know how much effort it takes you and you're looking more grumpy than usual today. Mitchell, I know you probably don't want to hear this, but you're nearing retirement and you have other commitments to think of now. I really think it is time for you to retire from teaching as soon as you can," says Marjorie earnestly.

Mitchell has his mouth full of toast, so he doesn't reply. He slurps on a cup of tea afterwards, then gets himself to his feet with the aid of his crutches. He manoeuvres himself out of the breakfast room with as much difficulty as he can without saying another word.

"Have a good day, Mitchell," says Marjorie leaving Mitchell to fumble around by the front door in the hallway to try and get himself onto his social-mobility scooter.

"Do you need some help out there?" asks Marjorie from the other room.

Mitchell mumbles and grumbles but she soon hears the scooter rev into power and it's not long after that that she hears the front door slam. She peeks out through the net curtains to watch her husband scooter away along the path towards the bus stop with his head held low and his face as miserable as sin. She giggles a little then returns to clearing away the breakfast dishes.

Mitchell Philpott picks up quite a speed on his social-mobility scooter as he drives haphazardly and carelessly as usual towards the bus stop at the end of his busy road. He can see a few other people waiting for the bus and that makes him keep his head low so that he can ignore them when he gets nearer.

Finally the bus draws up, late, by the side of the road allowing the other passengers to board as quickly as they can. The bus driver then rolls his eyes when he sees Mitchell Philpott aboard his social-mobility scooter, waiting at the bottom of the stairs of the bus to get aboard.

The bus driver is forced to press a button so that an aluminium lift can extend from out of the underside of the bus, near to a closed middle door in the centre. While the lift slowly lowers towards the ground, Mitchell manoeuvres himself nearer to it so that once the lift has lowered to the ground, he can drive onto it.

The passengers in the bus all begin to roll their eyes too, now, because the lift takes so long to lower to the ground. One impatient school boy gets to his feet and shouts, "Come on, old man!"

The aluminium lift finally lowers to the ground, the middle door opens and Mitchell drives his scooter onto the lift. One of the passengers then shouts to the driver to raise the lift, which the bus driver immediately does, unaware that one of the rear wheels of Mitchell's scooter has not driven onto the lift properly so that when the lift has risen to almost the level of the door of the bus, Mitchell's social-mobility scooter slides off the lift and falls down to the ground with a heavy crash that sends Mitchell flying off the scooter and onto the path near the bus stop.

"Oh, come on!" shouts another impatient passenger, when they look out of the window to find Mitchell Philpott lying on the ground, slumped over his scooter.

Fortunately, Mitchell is not hurt and in fact a sly smile appears over his face at the effect his scooter-driving skills are having on the irate passengers inside the bus. The bus driver is forced to get off the bus and help Mitchell get back onto his scooter and then onto the bus, which takes up more of the other passengers' valuable time.

The passengers are now well beyond rolling their eyes around with impatience. They are, instead, staring at Mitchell with anger, firmly believing that he has fallen off the lift purposely, which of course he hasn't, because Mitchell rarely falls off the bus lift more than once a week.

After a very heated and angry bus ride into the centre of town, Mitchell Philpott finally makes it into Honibridge Modern, still looking quite infirm, grumpy and still rarely able to rise his eyes from the ground for very long. He manoeuvres his social-mobility scooter along the school corridor, then into the woodwork room to find several of his pupils already at work at their benches.

The room is very compact and shelves on all sides are stacked high with all sorts of woodwork tools. Philpott has always had difficulty controlling his social-mobility scooter at the best of times, so when he tries to manoeuvre himself within the woodwork room, his problems become as acute as they were before he mysteriously disappeared one day last month, only to reappear later that night knocking on the door of his house so that his very worried wife could let him inside, but with no sign of his social-mobility scooter anywhere to be seen.

Marjorie has always been most keen for her husband to change his scooter, even after it was found under the bridge a few days ago. She feels it is far too powerful for him and he can't control it well enough.

Everyone at the school agrees with his wife, so when Mitchell drives his scooter straight into the legs of Ernest Thompson standing near to the entrance of the woodwork room, no one is surprised, least of all Thompson himself.

"Ouch!" cries Thompson, dropping a heavy piece of woodwork tooling onto the floor in the process.

Mitchell Philpott grumbles, then fiddles with his electronically controlled scooter without apologising for his actions and driving himself further into the woodwork room, much to the consternation of the other pupils around him.

"Watch out, Mr. Philpott!" cries Andrews, when Philpott reverses into the back of a woodwork bench, knocking into the shelving behind it and dislodging a heavy hand-plane that falls off its shelf, only narrowly missing Mitchell's head.

Philpott grumbles some more but he still does not seem too concerned by his dangerous driving, so he steers his mobile vehicle towards the front of the woodwork room with his face looking to the floor and his teeth bared in anger and dislike.

On his journey to the front of the classroom, Philpott manages to drive his scooter into the legs of almost every pupil he passes. He never apologises to any of them. He just looks to the scooter's electronic control panel, every now and again, as if to say his scooter does not work properly.

He finally reaches the front of the classroom, so that he can observe the whole class at work. It is his Year Elevens this morning, so they have important exam work to be getting on with. Philpott grumbles to himself before ever saying anything and he can see that Year Eleven's progress has been slow while he has been away.

"I hope you have all been working hard in my absence," says Philpott, plainly seeing they haven't. "From the undeveloped pieces of woodwork I have seen so far, this seems not to be the case," adds Philpott, grimacing because he has to open his mouth.

His pupils look back at him, feeling the same way about opening their mouths to reply.

"Now that I am back, I expect to see much harder and better work from all of you. Not long until the end of the school year and the examinations," adds Philpott, while he fiddles with his electronic driving device and reverses his scooter straight into the woodwork bench behind him, dislodging a heavy plane that sits on the highest shelf above, finally causing it to fall down towards his head.

Philpott sees the plane just in time. He nonchalantly throws a hammer that he's holding towards the wooden plane to knock it off its trajectory and prevent it from falling on his head. Philpott grumbles with satisfaction as the hammer carries on flying into the shelf higher up above his head, bringing down more woodwork tooling that then crashes onto the woodwork bench behind him.

He grumbles but once the crashing tools have quietened he returns to the pupils working ahead of him, intending to inspect their work more closely. However, unbeknown to him, there is still one heavy piece of woodwork equipment on the very topmost shelf that has been balancing precariously for several minutes. Only after things have quietened down below does it decide to fall off the shelf and head straight for Mitchell Philpott directly below it.

Philpott finally looks up at the falling piece of equipment but it is too late for him to do anything about it. The heavy implement is inches from his wide-eyed face, when Ben Andrews leans across the teacher's scooter to catch the heavy implement just before it hits Philpott in the face.

Andrews then calmly places the implement on the woodwork table and returns to his bench without saying anything. Philpott mumbles and grumbles under his breath but he is still in no mood to offer a word of thanks or an apology to any of his pupils, which is just about what Andrews is expecting.

The bell finally goes for the end of the lesson and his pupils have indeed upped their productivity, thanks to his presence. However, Mitchell Philpott does not give permission for any of his pupils to leave the woodwork room. It is left for Mitchell to fiddle with his electronic driving stick near to his hand, then manoeuvre himself back down through the narrow walkway, this time avoiding the pupils, and drive his scooter towards the school corridor, while his pupils watch him leave the room in ways that Philpott has no interest in trying to understand.

However, Philpott does not disappear out of the doorway as quickly as his pupils would like. He stops in the doorway of the woodwork room and with his back to his pupils suddenly sticks his tongue out then pulls his tongue quickly back into his mouth while tightening the skin around his mouth to bare his top set of teeth before finally straining the corners of his mouth downwards. Once he has finished this ritual, Philpott then manoeuvres his social-mobility scooter away along the corridor, leaving his pupils to look quite angrily towards the now-empty doorway.

Why Mr Philpott sticks his tongue out like this, no one is quite sure. It does look quite peculiar to anyone who hasn't met Mitchell Philpott before, yet everyone who is not new to the school is well used to the woodwork teacher performing this facial contortion several times a day, every day.

Some teachers consider it all an act, because Philpott's appearance throughout the whole ritual makes him appear very disgusted, at the time, with whatever he is doing. Perhaps he is disgusted, but with what, he never says. Perhaps he is disgusted with his pupils; perhaps he is disgusted with his fellow teachers; or perhaps he is just disgusted with the whole show but there is never a day when he does not perform this particular facial exercise and no one has found out the reason why he does it, nor indeed if he has any control over it.

Mitchell Philpott then grumbles his way along the corridor, probably because he's most irritated by the fact that almost everyone has now got used to this offensive gesture that he does purposely. Then again, maybe he grumbles because he still hasn't mastered his scooter that he continues to bump into the corridor walls and other pupils as he makes his way towards the staffroom. But one thing is always clear about Mitchell Philpott: he always looks grumpy, grumbly and sullen.

As Philpott nears the staffroom, Rose appears at the other end of the corridor behind him and as she hasn't spoken to him since his return to the school, she scampers along the corridor to catch up with him to help him steer a steadier course.

"Let me help you there, Mr. Philpott," says Rose, once she has caught up with him. She steadies his scooter while he continues to look downwards towards the floor, seemingly unhappy that she is helping him out.

Philpott grumbles continuously while Rose steers him straight ahead. We're almost treated to another one of his full gestures but Philpott manages to control it somehow and only bares his teeth at Rose this time, while she steadies his course.

"Nice to see you back in school, Mr. Philpott. You still need some lessons controlling this wayward scooter of yours, I see. I'll let the headmaster know. See what he can do," says Rose kindly.

Philpott face drops because he is forced to speak to her. "I don't need any more of those silly lessons," replies Philpott.

"Yes, that's what I often hear from many a woodwork pupil as well, Mr. Philpott," says Rose giggling, trying to lighten the mood. "I heard the good news, Mitchell, about you being promoted to the role of deputy mayor at the town hall a few weeks ago. Congratulations!" she adds.

"It was the wife's idea, all this mayoral stuff," replies Philpott, still grumbling.

"About you becoming deputy mayor? I didn't know you were married," says Rose, rather surprised. "She must know something we don't, Mr. Philpott," says Rose, still trying to lift Philpott's spirits.

Philpott can't stand any more of this friendly banter from Rose, so he fiddles with the scooter's control device and speeds away from her, mumbling and grumbling under his breath.

"Let's hope the mayor never takes a day off in the future," says Rose to herself, as Geoff catches up with her in the corridor.

"It works, Rose. The honey, it works!" says Geoff quietly to her when no one else can hear them.

"What do you mean, it works?" asks Rose, eyeing Geoff quite suspiciously then sighing.

"It's what we thought would happen if we took some of that honey, Rose. My Year Elevens: A or B-grade students now, every single one of them," says Geoff excitedly.

"I'm sorry, Geoff. I thought you just said that you had given some of Appleby's honey to your Year Eleven students. I must have been very mistaken. Good bye," replies Rose, trying to walk away from him. Geoff scampers up to her again. "You mean to say that you have actually tried some of that revolting honey in school, on the students!" cries Rose, looking quite disgusted.

"I do mean to say," replies Geoff.

"That really does take the biscuit, even for you," says Rose.

"I tried some of the honey last night. I knew it would work. I just knew it!" replies Geoff, still excitedly.

"I hope you realise that you can't use any more of it. That's it! Are the students okay? I will have to go to the headmaster or someone even higher if you ever try that again," says Rose angrily.

"We can't let this opportunity go to waste now. It worked just like we thought it would. All of the students got every answer in my lesson correct. Do you realise what we could achieve here? Do you realise what we could achieve for our headmaster?" replies Geoff, feeling quite hurt by Rose's rejection of his idea.

"There's no opportunity for us here, Geoff. And I don't like that glint in your eye," replies Rose, as the headmaster swoops around the corner of the corridor with his long, black gown billowing around his ankles.

"Geoff! Geoff, a word," says Anthony Bright when he spies them ahead. Rose does not want even to be seen with Geoff any more so she slopes away as quickly as she can, leaving Geoff to talk to the headmaster.

"I'm sorry I haven't had time to welcome you back, Geoff. I hope you have managed to sort out your issues. A nice clean fresh start and all that," says Bright, walking with him towards the staff room.

"I hope so, headmaster," replies Geoff.

"You know Rose was most insistent you start back as soon as possible. She's on your side, Geoff. When she can be. She's the one who's tried to influence me the most to get you back into the school and teaching again. Don't let her down now, will you, Geoff?" says Bright.

"I'll try not to," replies Geoff, now feeling slightly depressed.

"Some of the teachers here, including me, thought that perhaps a new start for you somewhere well away from here and perhaps away from Rose, as well, would have been the best option for you. Perhaps it still may be the best thing for you to do?" asks the headmaster.

"I am kind of settled around here in some ways," replies Geoff, knowing he could never leave this school while Rose was still here.

"Yes, that's what Rose has said about you, too, in a roundabout way. Now, I hope you can get your students back on track. We've had to delay Year Eleven's mocks while you've been away because of staffing issues, which I'm sure you knew about before your suspension anyway. They're going to be set in a few weeks' time so I'll leave you to arrange the maths mock exams. It'll mean a lot of cramming because the real things are only a few months away as it is," informs Bright.

"Right you are. I'll ramp up the workload. The students are going to love that," replies Geoff.

"I'll leave you to get on then," says Bright.

"Thanks, Anthony, I appreciate you bringing me back early," replies Geoff. The headmaster strides away urgently towards the staffroom, looking at his watch, to leave Geoff facing the unpleasant form of Max Heckton that now stands in the doorway of the staffroom waiting for his next prey. Heckton punches one of his fists into his other open hand, superhero-style, when he sees Geoff approach.

Geoff feels forced to change his lunchtime plans so he does not follow Bright into the staffroom. He walks on past the staffroom door and Max Heckton towards the front door of the school, hoping that Heckton does not say anything to him, which surprisingly he doesn't, this time.

Geoff emerges from the front door and makes his way through the school car park towards his small rental car, while the sun shines brightly above him on a coolish spring day in early March.

The throbbing of Roger Little's red Porsche soon disturbs what little peace there was to be found outside the confines of the school and it immediately grabs Geoff's attention. He watches Rose slope into the passenger seat of Roger's Porsche, on the other side of the car park, while she laughs excitedly.

Geoff tries frantically to open his car door with his keys so that he can avoid them when they drive past him but he can't find the right key. He soon realises that he is too late, because Roger's deep-sounding Porsche drives purposely slowly past Geoff so that he can easily see Rose sitting in his passenger seat.

Poor Geoff can't avoid looking at them. He feels forced to acknowledge them as they drive past and he can't help but look longingly towards Rose in the passenger seat, who purposely ignores him as they drive out of the school gates. Geoff finally opens the door of his rental car and climbs inside, feeling quite sad.

One evening, a few days later, Geoff wanders through one of Appleby's fields under a bright moon. He trips drunkenly over a wooden turnstile that separates two fields by a fence. He falls head-first into the field full of sleepy sheep. The sheep wake suddenly and start bleating loudly after being so rudely awoken.

Geoff quickly gets back to his feet, then staggers on towards Appleby's farmhouse at the far end of the field in front of him. He can see a light on inside the farmhouse kitchen, so he knocks on the kitchen door. There's no reply, so he grabs the door handle, opens the door, then stumbles inside.

He gasps with shock and hurt when he finds Appleby and Rose half undressed on the kitchen table. He can't believe his eyes at first and his poor heart can't handle it when he finally realises what he is seeing. His face drops even though he's very drunk.

"Rose! What are you doing here on your own?" cries Geoff.

"Geoff! Geoff, just the man!" shouts Appleby hastily removing himself from underneath Rose. He then pushes Rose towards the kitchen door while he buttons up his shirt.

"I'll come back," says Geoff, stumbling backwards towards the door.

"No, Geoff, you stay, Rose was just leaving," replies Appleby, doing up his trousers, while Rose creeps out of the kitchen door into the night without saying anything to Geoff.

Geoff slumps into the old chair in the corner of the kitchen, not sure how he'll be able to cope with things from now on. He finally manages to say what he came to the farmhouse to say.

"I thought you would like to know – your honey, it works. I tried some of it myself one evening, then tried it out on my students the next day," says Geoff, unhappily. "How long do the effects of the honey last for?" he adds.

"Yes, Rose was just telling me about what you did. That's what she came around to discuss. You know I'm not so sure using this honey on the school children is such a good idea," replies Appleby.

"That's Rose for you, putting a damper on things as usual," says Geoff. "Look, Russ, I'm convinced that if the students take some of this honey before their exams, they will become A or B-grade students, every single one of them. I'm telling you it works properly well," adds Geoff, now beginning to sob.

"So you're thinking that we should use this honey to help the students in their exams?" asks Appleby.

"Of course we should. Just think of the benefits to my career, to the future careers of all of my students," says Geoff excitedly.

Appleby's just about to say 'what's in it for me?', when he thinks better of it for the time being.

"You know that Rose doesn't agree with you? And she's told me that if you try using that stuff again, she'll tell on you," says Appleby. "That's what she came here to tell me," he adds, trying to make some kind of amends for his behaviour.

Geoff can contain it no longer. He begins to sob heavily. "What is it, Geoff?" asks Appleby.

Appleby takes a seat opposite Geoff while he continues to sob.

"You're more fond of Rose than I thought, aren't you, Geoff?" adds Appleby.

Chapter 9

Roger Little takes small purposeful steps towards the staffroom the next morning. He opens the staffroom door then scans the room for Rose. He finds her sulking in the corner, so he enters the room fully and walks over to her.

He can't contain his frustration any longer. "Just where were you last night? I couldn't get hold of you. Malcolm Purdy was very disappointed you didn't turn up. You're a vital cog in our team and we almost lost for the first time this season because you weren't there," he fumes to Rose.

Rose seems far too far away in her own thoughts to reply. When she finally comes round, she focuses on Roger's irate looking face.

"I can't believe you, Roger," says Rose. "Here I am, feeling very upset, and all you can think about is that silly bowls game," adds Rose.

"What's upsetting you this time?" asks Roger, rolling his eyes, then taking a seat next to her.

Rose's eyes well up with tears now she's got his attention. "What if I were to tell you I was with another man last night?" she replies.

"So you admit it now. You were with Geoff last night when you should have been playing bowls?" says Roger angrily.

"What if I were to tell you I was with another man and it wasn't Geoff," replies Rose, finally looking up to him.

A surprised then disgusted look appears over Roger's face. "I would say I don't believe you. You are nearly forty-five years old and not ageing well," replies Roger.

Rose cries a little when she hears this. "That's not very nice of you, Roger," says Rose, glancing to one side to see the other seated teachers nearby quickly try to find something else to look at and talk about.

"You know, don't you?" asks Rose.

"Know what?" asks Roger, now not caring a fig about the other teachers listening in.

"Aghh!" cries Rose, getting up to move Roger somewhere more private.

Roger is not putting up with any more of her nonsense. He walks away from her, too disgusted that she wasn't at the bowls club last night to stay and talk with her here.

"Where are you going?" asks Rose.

"I'm a teacher, Rose. I've got a class to teach," replies Roger, walking out of the staffroom to avoid more glaring eyes and leaving Rose to slump back into her seat to resume her sulk.

As she sulks, there is something that Rose sees out of the corner of her eye that makes her look towards the other corner of the staffroom. She finds Max Heckton staring at her and baring his teeth, while punching one of his fists into his other open hand, superhero-style, obviously delighted by the open confrontation he has just witnessed between Rose and Roger in the staffroom. Rose looks at him with disgust and tries to hide her face in a tissue she's been holding.

A little later into the same school day, Geoff closes the door to his empty classroom and strides away, carrying his backpack full of books over one of his shoulders.

He walks along the seemingly empty corridor when he suddenly feels himself being pushed against the wall of the corridor. Geoff is shaken but he instantly knows who's pinned him against the side of the wall, even before he's managed to focus on the ugly, snarling and hissing face that appears right in front of his.

Max Heckton pushes Geoff's head back against the wall, then hisses like a snake quite loudly into Geoff's held face.

"Wade, Wade, Wade. What am I going to do with you?" says Heckton as he hisses some more.

"You're going to let me out of this head-grip to start with. We're not in the desert or wherever you and Bright were. I've found out about that. This is a school, in case you hadn't noticed. You can't attack teachers like this and expect to get away with it," replies Geoff, being as reasonable as he can, given the circumstances.

"I don't agree with you," says Heckton menacingly, while tightening his grip on him.

"You don't agree with anyone," replies Geoff, struggling to breathe.

"Do I need a reason to pin your head against this wall?" asks Heckton.

"I would say you do if you want to stay working here," replies Geoff, finally feeling a slight loosening of Heckton's grip.

"I would say I don't," says Heckton hissing into Geoff's face. "I've heard about your little stunt with Year Nine's geography books and if it turns out to be true, which even I can't see you actually doing, then the headmaster will be the first to know about it," adds Heckton.

"Teacher camaraderie is a wonderful thing," replies Geoff.

"I've already told the headmaster about what I think happened to those geography books and you should be in serious trouble, yet somehow you don't seem to be. And as you know I don't like that. I don't like people not being in trouble with the headmaster," says Heckton.

"Heckton, I can't breathe," squeals Geoff as Heckton's forced to loosen his grip some more.

"Something's going on, Wade; I know something's going on. I can smell it in the air and there's a funny smell about you. I don't like it. I'm going to find out what it is you are up to and I'm going to put you in a whole world of trouble with the headmaster," says Heckton, peering into Geoff's eyes while Geoff's head is still pinned against the wall.

"If only the headmaster could hear and see you now," replies Geoff, feeling faint.

"There's talk that you're improving your Year Eleven's maths grades. I can't believe there are any A or B-grade students in any of your classes!" says Heckton incredulously.

"What can I say? I've turned things around. I'm a new man. Can't you tell?" replies Geoff, feeling his sore neck.

"I don't like that smell I can smell when I'm around you, Wade. The headmaster seems to like you as much as I don't like you. What's your secret?" asks Heckton.

"If you let me get away from this wall, I will tell you," replies Geoff.

Heckton finally releases his grip on Geoff and moves away from him. Geoff then breathes in some large gasps of air before pulling Heckton's legs out from out under him, causing him to fall to the ground.

Geoff then lifts Heckton from the floor holding his shirt collars and return hisses into Heckton's face.

"You try that one more time, Heckton, and I will put you so deep into trouble that you won't be able to see the light at the top of the well," says Geoff angrily.

Heckton gets to his feet, feeling slightly shaken by Geoff's countermove so he pushes Geoff against the corridor wall once more. Geoff's anger now boils over and as he grabs Heckton's head, Heckton does likewise, forcing them both to grip each other in head locks that eventually brings them both to the floor, where they writhe around in a seemingly unbreakable tussle.

Neither one of them seems keen to relent, so when Ernest Thompson and Ben Andrews walk around the corner of the corridor to find these two teachers tussling on the floor, it is left to them to try and break it up.

"Mr Wade! Are you okay?" asks Andrews.

"That's enough you two, break it up!" says Thompson, too afraid to enter the fray and pull them apart.

The two tussling teachers do not hear them and it takes several more snake-like hisses from both of them to scare Andrews into action.

"I'll go and get help," says Andrews, keen to get away from the situation.

It is left to Geoff to first notice the two pupils standing above them, as he gasps for air.

"I'll go and get the headmaster," says Thompson, keen to get away, too.

"No!" says Geoff desperately, as Thompson's words finally scare both of them into action, allowing him to pull himself free of Heckton's grip, stand up and then straighten his tie.

Heckton gets to his feet just as quickly, which leaves both of them feeling quite uncomfortable in the company of the two students in the corridor. Heckton soon huffs, then walks away along the corridor leaving Geoff to walk away in the opposite direction, without either of them saying anything more to Andrews and Thompson.

Once Geoff has turned the corner of the corridor, he leans against the wall to catch his breath. "Heckton really is the most unpleasant person I've ever met," says Geoff to himself, just before several more students walk around the corner of the corridor forcing him to remove himself from the wall and act like a decent and sensible teacher once again.

One evening, a few days later, Rose and Roger find themselves under the bowls club floodlights. The glare beams down over the immaculately repaired bowls green, as several matches play simultaneously across the large lawn surface.

Rose crouches with a bowl in her hand, then releases it with a finesse and expertise that even Malcolm Purdy, standing at the edge of the green, quietly admires and respects. Rose's bowl goes on to hit an opponent's bowl clear away from the jack, then nestle as close to the jack as it is possible to nestle. Roger immediately applauds her heartily, knowing that he could hardly have played a better shot.

"Bravo, Rose!" shouts Purdy from the sidelines, while he turns the hefty gold ring on his left middle finger rather nervously.

"Good bowling, my dear!" shouts Roger. "That wraps up the win, I think?" he says to the captain of the opposing team. The opposing captain peruses the bowls on the green to tot up the scores himself and looks to the scoreboard, just to make sure Roger's maths skills are correct, then he shakes Roger's hand heartily, knowing that he has never been outplayed that well in many a year.

"I concur," says the captain of the other team, while applause rings out around the bowls green and muffled applause seeps through the tinted-glass frontage of the bowls club behind them.

Malcolm Purdy strides onto the green with his hands in the air and his gold rings glistening under the almost blinding floodlights. He heartily shakes the hand of the captain of the visiting team for being such a gallant loser, then goes over to Rose to pat her vigorously on the back.

He's unable to contain his excitement for Rose, his new star player. He feels that he has personally discovered her and brought her into their impressive county-winning team and so, in many ways, he believes he is responsible for tonight's triumph.

Purdy then quite deliberately puts his hand around the waist of Roger Little to congratulate him, too, as they make their way off the bowls green and head towards the tinted-glass frontage of the bowls club.

Roger tries to move himself clear of Purdy but Purdy's hefty, gold-ring-covered hand holds Roger quite firmly in place right next to him. As they approach the clubhouse, the applause wafts over the bowls green from the remaining matches that have yet to be completed. Their opponents eventually close in on the home team's advantage but it still doesn't quite provide them with enough points to move ahead of Purdy's prize winners.

Once the win is confirmed, half a dozen bowls supporters rush out of the bowls club to congratulate Purdy on another successful season. This causes Purdy to reluctantly remove his hand from around Roger's waist, so that he can shake all of their eager hands.

Purdy's tall and charismatic figure stands head and shoulders above the rest of the players and supporters as they pass him by to enter the clubhouse. He's certainly the leader of the pack in this corner of Honibridge and he has been for many a year.

Malcolm Purdy is a legend, some would say; perhaps the most influential bowls player to come out of this neck of the woods in living memory, say others, not least his second-in-command, Bill Richards, who has also been at the bowls club since the mists of time first rolled across this particular bowls-green lawn, as far back as the 1970s.

The winning smiles and pats on the backs from the bowls players of both teams soon leads into a right old booze-up inside the bowls club. Roger and Rose are toasted for their excellent display out on the green earlier and as they take drinks inside the bowls club, they chat as enthusiastically about their win as their fellow team mates, most of whom have been at the club for almost as long as Purdy himself.

Later into the evening, Malcolm Purdy approaches the toasted pair through the crowded bar, this time looking far from sober. Yet Rose can still see a presence about him that tells her that he's the leader of the pack around here.

Some of the lesser players at the bowls club have said to her that his charisma has always trumped his actual bowling abilities, which may have possibly become slightly jaded since the heady days of his bowling prowess in the late 1990s and the early years of the twenty-first century. Yet, to Rose, there's no mistaking a legend of the game as he approaches her through the throng of excited and drunken sports enthusiasts.

Being quite drunk, too, and unable to control her actions, Rose wafts her hand through the air when Purdy approaches, to try and clear the air of his very potent-smelling aftershave that's strong enough to make Roger cough a little when the fumes hit the back of his throat. Her actions would have usually caused offence to Purdy but this night, even Purdy will forgive her for her error.

Purdy greets them with a wide and drunken, teeth-baring grin.

"That aftershave, Malcolm – I'm not familiar with it," says Roger diplomatically, still coughing and unable to hide it.

"I thought I would treat myself. It's for special occasions such as this, you understand. It took me a good shop to find this particular brand. I was surprised when I found it; I didn't think they stocked it in this country," replies Purdy.

"Why, is it illegal over here?" asks Roger causing Rose to chuckle.

"Do you like it, too, Roger?" asks Purdy.

"Not my particular brand, I'm afraid," replies Roger.

"I'm trying to make Roger cut down on his aftershave," adds Rose.

"Yes, Rose is right, I'm not really an aftershave sort of person anyway," says Roger.

"Oh, that is a shame, Roger. Now, Rose, there's been great talk about your skills on the bowls lawn. Someone's even had the nerve to compare your skills on the bowling green with mine," says Purdy, drinking down a pint of lager in one gulp.

"With you? The great Malcolm Purdy? I can't believe it," replies Rose, feeling quite lightheaded.

"Yes, please believe it, Rose," says Purdy. "I agree with them in some respects, especially these days.

You've got a real cutting-edge winners eye and you proved it tonight. I was impressed" adds Purdy.

"Me? Cutting edge? Surely not," replies Rose.

"Almost all of the rest of the team have commented on your skills. I can't remember anyone making quite so big an impression in their first season," says Purdy.

"You really think so?" replies Rose, trying to guess the combined cost of all those hefty gold rings Purdy wears on every finger of each hand.

"You're a natural, Rose, and a handsome couple you both make. We're delighted you've both been such a huge success here," says Purdy, polishing off another whole pint of lager in one go.

"I'm glad to hear it. It's not very often we get such praise like that, is it Rose? That it should come from the local bowls club, too," replies Roger.

"There are a few of us are going back to my place later on and we would love you both to join us," says Purdy, eyeing Rose's slim figure.

"I'm not sure about that, Malcolm," says Rose, very aware of Purdy's lustful eyes.

"Yes, it's a school night you know. It is a school night, isn't it, Rose?" asks Roger.

Purdy's eyes then move from Rose to ogle Roger in an equally lustful manner. He moves much closer to Roger. "Well, perhaps you could both come back just this once then. You're both welcome to stay over. I'm sure my wife won't mind sleeping in the spare room," says Purdy, licking his lips.

"Aghhh, we should be going, Roger," says Rose putting her half-finished brandy glass onto the bar.

"Yes, a busy day tomorrow and all that," says Roger, spilling his pint to avoid Purdy's lustful eyes.

Rose grabs Roger's arm, then hauls him out through the excited and half-drunk group of bowls players, who all frown at the pair of them for rejecting Malcom Purdy's advances. Even some of the visiting team's players open their mouths with shock, when they find out that Roger and Rose have had the temerity to reject Purdy in that way.

Roger and Rose have difficultly making their way through the crowded bar towards the door for this reason and several members of his team look towards Purdy at the bar for some kind of signal to restrain them both before they get away.

Purdy himself, since being rejected by the escaping pair, continues to look at the space where Roger and Rose once stood without moving a muscle, because he's that stunned by their rejection and you get the feeling that he has never, ever before been rejected like this.

His cheeks turns a deep purple colour as he becomes too embarrassed to reveal his face to the other members of his bowls team, so he stares at the wall near to the bar without being able to turn to face them. Purdy's lack of response allows Roger and Rose to finally squeeze through the last of the very offended bowls players, then quickly exit through the swinging front door of the bowls club.

Roger's Porsche throbs and cruises through the night as he drives along a winding country lane following the events of the evening at the bowls club. Roger remains quiet, while Rose sits quietly next to him, leaving him to follow the bright headlights of his car that shine into the far distance quite a long way ahead. Roger is feeling slightly drowsy from the pint of lager he had drunk at the bowls club and from the tiring effects of the stressful bowls game that they have just won.

Roger's attention is suddenly grabbed by something dark that moves ahead of his car to one side in the field next to them. His car's headlights illuminate the field, dimly making out the dark, moving object that stays in Roger's view. Roger straightens himself up in his seat to focus more on the movement to the left of his car. He still can't see anything on the lane ahead of him, so he slows his car down to have a proper look out of Rose's window to see if he can make out what is moving out there.

He can't see anything through Rose's window so he looks more closely through his front windscreen, while he drives his car at walking pace so that he can identify what captured his attention moments earlier should it appear again, but all he can see is darkness, until–

"Aghhh!" cries Rose suddenly, next to him, when Russell Appleby's astonished face appears immediately ahead of them in the lane, then disappears back into the darkness of the field on the other side just as quickly.

"Did you see that? Did you see him?" cries Roger excitedly.

"Russell Appleby! I'm sure it was Russell Appleby!" cries Rose. "What's he doing in the field this late at night?" asks Rose, looking to Roger for answers.

Roger doesn't know so he doesn't reply. He continues to drive his car at walking pace along the winding country lane, half expecting Appleby to jump out of the trees in front of them at any minute.

"Who was that and what on earth was he doing out here at this hour?" asks Roger finally.

Rose doesn't want to say too much about Appleby to Roger if she can help it.

"I can't be sure but I think that could have been the farmer that owns the fields around here," says Rose.

"How would you know that?" asks Roger, still straining to see through the windscreen into the night.

"I've seen him before, I think. I think these are his fields, but I can't be sure," replies Rose.

Roger soon tires of the search out of the window so he takes Rose's word on the subject to be the answer. He has almost lost interest in the jumping figure until the pale moon lights over the dark, moving object of Russell Appleby in the distance near to the top of a hill.

Roger's forced to slam on the brakes of his car to observe the phenomenon as best he can. He can now clearly see the figure jumping as high as a house away through the fields on the other side of the lane and it makes Roger's mouth drop open with shock.

"Great balls of fire. . . There's a man jumping through that field over there and he's jumping as high as a house," exclaims Roger.

"Oh, how can you be so silly, Roger. It's a school night. Nobody jumps through a field like that on a school night," replies Rose.

"I'm serious, Rose. Whoever he was, he was leaping so high it almost seemed like he was flying," says Roger, parking his car on a mud-made lay-by on the side of the lane.

"It's Malcolm Purdy," replies Rose.

"No, it wasn't Malcolm Purdy. How could that have been him? But you could be right about it being that farmer," says Roger.

"Russell Appleby," replies Rose.

"Russell Appleby? Is that his name?" asks Roger.

"That's the name of the farmer's son and I'm pretty sure that was him," replies Rose.

"Whoever it was, that's not the point. He was jumping so high. Didn't you see him?" asks Roger.

Rose feels drunk and exhausted and has no interest in Appleby's antics in the field any more. She's also keen to avoid any more discussions about him as much as possible.

"Why did you think it was Malcolm Purdy jumping through those fields?" asks Roger.

"Malcolm Purdy's got you stressed out. You're thinking about things too much again, which I've told you about before. You're seeing things that aren't there," replies Rose, while Roger pulls himself out of his car to take a better look into the field under the pale moon.

Roger soon picks up the jumping, dark object now at the very top of the hill and he watches on, open-mouthed, while Appleby jumps high away through the field into the darkness of the night.

"That really was most extraordinary," says Roger, still not able to fathom what he has just witnessed. Once the jumping figure has finally disappeared, Roger slopes back into the driver's seat of his Porsche.

"That really was most unusual, Rose. I've never seen the like of it before," says Roger.

"It was probably a jumping deer," replies Rose. "They can jump really high when they're distressed," she adds.

"No, that was no jumping deer. That was a man doing the jumping. Whether it was this farmer's son, Russell Appleby, I don't know. But that surely isn't the point, Rose. Most extraordinary, how can someone jump that high?" says Roger, slapping his face on one side to make sure he's still awake.

"And on a school night, too," replies Rose.

"Russell Appleby? Yes, I do know that name, I think. He's a member of the university science club if I'm correct, which I invariably am," replies Roger, while he looks to Rose sitting next to him. "That was definitely no deer, my dear," adds Roger, sensing that she has something to hide from him.

Roger then looks at her more closely. "You didn't seem at all surprised to see Russell Appleby or whoever it was jumping through the fields like that," says Roger.

Rose remains quiet. She knows she has already said too much. "Can we get moving again? School tomorrow don't forget," she replies, finally.

"You know him, don't you? I can tell, Rose. You're hiding something from me. How do you know him, Rose? How do you know this Russell Appleby?" questions Roger.

Rose remains reluctant to speak. "I don't know him. Maybe, perhaps, Geoff introduced me to him one time. I don't really remember him if he did," replies Rose.

"He's one of Geoff's acquaintances? My God, Rose – he's the other man, isn't he," says Roger instinctively. Rose remains quiet. "So, you have been seeing someone! My God, Rose, you're almost forty-six years old!" says Roger not quite believing it could be possible. "There I was, thinking the only other person in the world who would have had you was Geoff, then I find out you've been seeing someone else, too; not least the local farmer who goes wild-jumping through the fields of a night," says Roger irately.

"I don't know what you're talking about, Roger. Now, please can you take me home. I'm feeling very drunk and very tired," says Rose quite urgently.

"No, I'm sure of it now. I can tell you know him better than that. You're blushing. You've gone all defensive," replies Roger.

Rose begins to cry. "Oh, Roger, I needed some company. You can be so– so. . . sensible at times. You're always talking about work and. . . and. . ." says Rose hesitatingly.

"What is it, Rose?" asks Roger, staring at her now.

"You're not even good at it. You're not even a good teacher," says Rose, trying to change the subject as quickly as possible but realising she's making things worse for herself every time she speaks.

"I say, that's a bit harsh, Rose. In fact, that's very harsh of you. I work very hard at my teaching, I'm the deputy head of my department, Rose. I have a lot of work to keep up on, you know that. I told you that when we first started going out," says Roger.

"It's just that I need you to kiss me, to hug me, even just some of the time. You hardly do that at all, or only when I prompt you," replies Rose, with tears in her eyes.

"So, you have been seeing this. . . Russell Appleby," replies Roger leaning over to open her passenger door.

"What are you doing?" asks Rose.

"You've been rude to me; you've criticised my teaching. And then you have the nerve to tell me you're seeing someone else," says Roger.

Rose cries again, while Roger looks at her, feeling annoyed. "You see, this is something we have discussed before, Rose," adds Roger.

"What have we discussed before, Roger?" asks Rose.

"I've told you to stop being so emotional all the time and yet you still persist in this rather childish behaviour. I told you, when we started going out, that you needed to be a bit more grown up and responsible now that you were going out with a senior teacher at the school," says Roger.

Rose laughs through her tears. "You see, this is what I'm talking about and no one seems to have spoken to you about it," replies Rose.

"Spoken to me about what?" says Roger.

"Spoken to you about your teaching," says Rose, in half a mind as to whether to continue with this line of argument, given the circumstances, but she is so upset that she carries on, anyway. "You're in no way the best English teacher, even at this school," adds Rose.

"What do you mean? I'm deputy head of the English department. I don't think you get to that position by being a slouch or not working at it," says Roger.

"But as a teacher, I mean. There's Valerie Coutt – she's a way better English teacher than you," replies Rose.

"Valerie Coutt? Yes, well, Valerie Coutt – there's probably very few better at our art than Valerie Coutt," says Roger.

"And then there are the others. In fact. . ." replies Rose, still not convinced she should go on. "There are all of the other English teachers at our school. I wouldn't put you at the bottom of the pile, Roger, because of your hard work and your seniority," replies Rose, pleased she has finally got all of this out in the open.

"That's so harsh, Rose. It's all I live for, my teaching. And then you go and say something like this," says Roger, while he leans over to open her passenger door again. "Get out, Rose," he adds, angrily.

"You can't ask me to get out here," replies Rose.

"I can and I am. My girlfriend first tells me she's seeing someone else and then she goes and says something like this to me. It's very hurtful of you and I don't think we can go on," says Roger.

Rose sobs a little. "I'm sorry, Roger, that was a bit harsh of me, I apologise. I wish I could be as grown up about things as you," replies Rose.

Roger feels a little calmed and knows he can't just leave Rose out here in the middle of the fields. "I'm a teacher, Rose. I teach things, regardless of what you think about my teaching. A teacher has to be grown up about things, all things," says Roger, making Rose feel guilty about her misdemeanours.

Rose closes her car door quietly and stays in her seat. "Yes, Roger. I'll try to behave more like a grown up in the future," replies Rose, pleased she has managed to deflect away her errant ways with this rather hurtful counter attack on Roger's teaching abilities, as well as discovering that Roger seems to like being called a grown up.

"You certainly will have to try to be more of a grown up in the future if you want to carry on going out with me. In case you hadn't noticed, you're a teacher, too, Rose," says Roger.

"I know, Roger. It's just that sometimes I find it hard to be as grown up as you, like most people would," replies Rose.

"Yes, well, that's why I'm deputy head of my department and you're not. Which is something you should certainly be aiming for now, given your age. A teacher can't just switch off being a teacher when he or she feels like it. A teacher is a teacher, twenty-four hours a day, seven days a week, whether they're in school, in the library, or even at the train station. Do you understand me, Rose?" explains Roger.

"I'm always trying to, Roger, and sometimes I do think I understand you very well. You are such a mature specimen of manhood and I want to be more like you, I really do, providing you bear in mind that I'm only a year older than you," replies Rose, while Roger starts up his throbbing Porsche once more.

Roger then scans the fields on both sides of the road, just to check that there are no more people jumping through them and once he's completely satisfied that this is indeed the case, he drives his car back onto the country lane.

"That's very sensible of you, Rose. Let's have no more of this emotional nonsense that you sometimes drift into for no apparent reason. I often wonder if you wouldn't be better off with Geoff. He's an emotional wreck most of the time, just like you. If we're going to move our relationship forward, you'll need to start behaving more maturely. If there's one thing I can't stand it is immaturity," explains Roger.

"Oh yes, Roger. Yes, yes, please – let's move our relationship forward," says Rose, not completely convinced by her words.

Roger pushes the accelerator right down to speed his Porsche along the winding country lane, because he's feeling slightly angry by Rose's harsh words. He's also determined not to dwell on them any longer.

"That really was most unusual," says Roger to himself more than anything, when he ponders the jumping night owl that he has just witnessed in the fields.

They both remain silent for the rest of the journey for they both know that that would be for the best for the time being. Roger's powerful light-beamed Porsche throbs its way along the winding country lane until its lights disappear from view under some heavy trees, leaving the throb of the engine to echo through the countryside, long after the rear lights have disappeared from sight.

Chapter 10

Geoff walks swiftly along one of the corridors of the school towards his classroom. He can hear Max Heckton's strict words echo through a door he passes, so he jumps rapidly onwards along the corridor to avoid hearing anything more from him.

He opens the door to his classroom and quickly notices the empty beakers of honeyed blackcurrant juice on a tray on his desk at the front of the classroom.

He strides over to some trigonometry diagrams that he drew earlier on the board behind his desk. Geoff smiles knowingly as he peruses the diagrams on the board.

"So, how are we doing, class?" asks Geoff. "Ben Andrews?"

"A-squared equals B-squared plus C-squared, minus 2BC Cosine A," replies Andrews, confidently.

"Very good, Andrews," says Geoff. "Now, did everyone else get the right equation to use on this little question?" he asks.

The class reply in sober union as one.

"Yes, sir," they all say.

"Twenty-three degrees," booms Ernest Thompson from the back of the classroom.

"I was just going to ask if anyone had managed to get around to calculating the answer and the answer seems to be yes. Twenty-three degrees, you say?" says Geoff looking up the answer in the back of his book.

"Is the correct answer," adds Geoff happily. "Did anyone else get the correct answer?" he asks.

"Yes, sir," replies the whole class once more.

"Very good again then, class," replies Geoff. "Now, let's continue with these questions in your text book and work your way to the bottom of the page," says Geoff, smiling as he takes a seat at his desk, quite satisfied that they have now learnt what they should have learnt by this stage of the year, given the mocks are now very near.

Now that he's given the class their instructions, Geoff's almost ready to take a quick shuteye as it's late in the afternoon and near to the end of the school day. However, there is one pupil in the class ahead of him who looks far from settled. He notices Ernest Thompson looking out of the window at something that catches his attention quite urgently outside.

Thompson stares out of the window with his eyes wide open with wonder, forcing Geoff to unsettle the status quo.

"What is it, Thompson?" asks Geoff, feeling quite concerned. Then he notices Ben Andrews at the desk in front of Thompson stare out of the window, too, with his eyes wide with wonder.

"Goodness gracious, sir," says Thompson, still staring out of the window. "In the field over there, look!" adds Thompson, getting to his feet and moving closer to the window.

"I see him, too!" cries Andrews, jumping over to the window.

Geoff scrambles out of his chair, fearing the worst, then strides over to the window the two boys are looking out of. His fears are confirmed when he catches a glimpse of Russell Appleby jumping enormous jumps through the field on the other side of the school playing fields.

"You others remain in your seats," says Geoff, when he hears several of the other students behind him scramble out of their chairs to take a look.

"Can you see him? In those fields over there. It looks like a man is almost flying through that field!" exclaims Thompson.

Geoff can see Appleby jumping through the fields on the other side of the school and he's not sure what to do or what to say.

"I can see him, too! He's jumping as high as the school all the way through those fields!" says an astonished Andrews.

"That is most extraordinary, sir. I've never seen such an oddity and I come to this school every day," adds Thompson.

"How can someone fly like that without wings or something?" asks Sarah Jordan, unable to resist running over to another window to take a look.

"Yeah, without wings and without any kind of machine attached to his body," adds Andrews.

To Geoff's relief, Appleby soon disappears from view from the school windows.

"That certainly was an oddity, sir," adds Thompson. "Did you see him, sir?" he asks.

"See who?" replies Geoff, knowing only too well that Thompson and Andrews had seen him witness Appleby almost fly through those distant fields.

Geoff is about to send Thompson, Andrews and Jordan back to their seats, when he notices something else capture his attention in the far corner of the playing fields, near to a large oak tree.

"Now, you three, return to your seats," says Geoff looking quite concerned. Thompson, Andrews and Jordan reluctantly return to their desks looking slightly disappointed.

Geoff stays at the window to observe the behaviour that concerns him greatly near to the mature oak tree in the playing fields outside. From what he can make out, from where he is, Max Heckton pins Anthony Bright's head to the trunk of the oak tree in a very threatening manner.

Geoff quickly whisks himself over to the door of the classroom. "Now, class – continue with those questions in your exercise book. I will be back in a minute," says Geoff.

"I hope you're going to explain how that man jumped through that field like that when you get back, with diagrams to explain it?" asks Thompson.

"Just continue with your exercises," says Geoff.

"But I didn't bring my shorts into school today, sir," replies Andrews.

"I'm serious, guys, the mocks are next week and there's still more we need to cram in. You've done very well getting to where you are but don't let up now, we're so close," says Geoff.

Andrews furrows his brow, all serious-like, while he stares into his exercise book, just before Geoff closes the classroom door behind him.

Geoff whisks himself along the school corridor until he stands outside the headmaster's office. He then knocks on the headmaster's door, after following the headmaster back inside the school from the playing fields.

"Who is it?" asks Bright curtly.

"Geoff Wade," replies Geoff.

"Oh. Oh, come in then," says Bright, more calmly.

Geoff tentatively enters the headmaster's office. He finds Bright sitting behind his desk looking quite worried. Geoff notices Bright's hands shake as he pours himself a whisky. Bright gulps down the whisky in one go without offering Geoff a glass. The headmaster then briefly puts his hands over his face and rubs. He can tell that Geoff noticed his shaking hands.

"Are you all right, Anthony?" asks Geoff.

"Oh, it's Heckton," replies the headmaster, guessing that Geoff saw his little set-to with Heckton in the playing fields just now. "He's always been a live wire; difficult to control, if you know what I mean," says Bright as Geoff takes a seat.

"You're telling me. He looked very wired out there just now. Even more wired than usual and he's pretty wired most of the time," replies Geoff. "What's he got on you?" he asks, almost knowing that Bright won't tell him.

"Oh, oh – it's personal. Nothing to do with you," replies Bright.

"Perhaps I might suggest the cane, sir? That should put him in his place," says Geoff, almost seriously. Bright immediately gets up from his seat, then nervously eyes the closed door behind Geoff as if to say *you can go now*.

"You can't let Heckton threaten you like that. I saw the whole thing from my classroom. He's a nasty piece of work, regardless of what happened in the desert between you two. He shouldn't be working at this school," says Geoff.

Bright immediately takes offence and Geoff is quick to pick up that he's lucky to still be working at the school, too. Geoff remains quiet for a moment.

"Do you think I'm going to discuss this matter with you? I can sort out my own problems, thank you very much," replies Bright.

Geoff gets up from his seat. He has said too much and he knows it. "Just as long as you do sort things out. I know what Heckton's like, you know," replies Geoff, walking towards the door.

Bright's hands still shake as he moves towards the window. "You will keep what you just saw in the playing fields between us two? Don't mention Heckton to anyone else, will you?" says Bright, looking away from him.

"I will keep it between us," says Geoff, as he closes the office door behind him.

Later that evening, Geoff drives his newly bought second-hand car onto the gravel driveway of Appleby's farmhouse. He turns off the ignition of the battered-looking car, then steps outside. He slams the car door closed to make sure it shuts properly, which this time causes the car to reignite its engine back into life and make the car jump forward a little before turning itself off and going quiet again.

Geoff strides through the darkness towards Appleby's farmhouse kitchen door. He pushes it wide open to find Appleby and Rose, once more, half naked on the kitchen table. When she sees Geoff enter the kitchen, Rose quickly slopes away from under Appleby and picks up her clothes from the floor, leaving Appleby to remove himself from the table as quickly as he can and straighten himself up while doing up his shirt buttons.

"We must stop meeting like this," says Geoff, feeling once more heartbroken.

"Shouldn't you wait until someone answers the door, Geoff?" says Rose angrily.

"It's more fun this way," replies Geoff.

"You should really call me first if you're going to come around, Geoff. I may not be in," says Appleby.

"We need to talk," replies Geoff.

"We certainly do. Take a seat," says Appleby.

"Russell?" asks Rose as she stands nervously by the kitchen door not sure whether she should go or stay.

"Now that you're here, Rose, I need to talk to both of you," says Geoff taking a chair at the kitchen table, feeling quite upset.

"Some of my students in school saw you jumping through those fields this afternoon, Russell. What do you think you're playing at, jumping around near to the school?" asks Geoff.

"Yes, Russell, that's what I came round to tell you, too. Roger and I saw you jumping through some of your fields a few nights ago. I thought it must have been you," adds Rose.

"We three are going to get found out if you carry on like this. And I, for one, cannot afford to get found out. You know what sort of risk I'm taking with this honey business," says Geoff irately.

"Calm down, Geoff. No one's going to get found out," replies Appleby. "You didn't tell anyone it was me who was doing the jumping did you?" he asks.

Rose coughs nervously. "I may have said something to Roger. I can't remember really," says Rose.

"You did what?" replies Appleby, staring at her.

"I may have said something about it being the farmer from around these parts. I may have said your name but I can't really remember and it was dark anyway, so it could have been anyone," says Rose, quite honestly.

"I can't believe you told him my name! I told you both – all of this must be kept between the three of us," replies Appleby. "Why did you tell him that?"

"I can't really remember, maybe I didn't tell him. I was upset," says Rose.

"And let's not forget that it was actually you jumping through the fields," adds Geoff.

"What do you mean by that?" replies Appleby

"I mean that if you hadn't been jumping through the fields, you wouldn't have been seen jumping through those fields," adds Geoff.

"It was dark. That's when I try out this synthesised honey. So that no one can see me doing it," replies Appleby.

"And yesterday? During the day when you were near to the school?" asks Geoff.

"Yes, well. . ." replies Appleby.

"'Yes, well' what?" asks Geoff.

"All I'm saying is that the honey works more often than not, depending on when you take it," replies Appleby.

"You mean to tell me that it doesn't always work the way it should?" asks Geoff, ready to tear out his hair.

Appleby remains silent for a moment. "What were you upset about yesterday, Rose?" says Appleby finally.

"I don't know, probably something Roger did, that's all," replies Rose.

"The point is, Russell, you shouldn't be jumping through these fields any more at all, day or night," says Geoff.

"I'm afraid I have to," replies Appleby, making himself a coffee.

"Because the honey's not as reliable as we thought?" asks Geoff.

"I'm saying that the honey works as it should do most of the time but it still needs research. I've been trying to find out as much as I can about it so that we can synthesise the honey properly and know for certain what it will do and when. And that's why I do the testing on myself, mostly at night, to learn more about it. Look, Geoff, if we're going to make a success of this venture, we must know as much as we can about it," says Appleby convincingly.

"What are you two up to? What have you agreed?" asks Rose worried. "I came here to tell you, Russell, that you can't use this honey on the students any more if that's what you are intending," adds Rose.

"Rose, I need to clarify with you what we intend to do. Russell and myself have agreed that we're going to use this honey on the students because we're going to improve their exam results. They need our help because with so many of our teachers at our school being suspended or going awol, we need to give them a boost and this is the perfect way to help them," explains Geoff.

"I see, but after what Russell has just told you, you can't go ahead with your little plan. It might not work and it might send all of the students jumping away through the fields or even something worse. It can't go any further now and that's final. I knew you two would be up to something. I can't believe it! I will have to tell the headmaster first thing tomorrow morning. You can't be allowed to get away with this sort of behaviour any longer!" cries Rose irately.

"It's worked every time in school so far," replies Geoff, half expecting this kind of reaction from Rose.

"And it will be the last time you will use this honey on the students in our school. Have you got that? Both of you?" replies Rose, in her strictest teacher's voice.

"That's why I've been working on the solution. My research has synthesised the properties of the honey. It has to be an exact quantity given to each of the students if they are going to benefit the most from it," replies Appleby.

"You mean to say that I have just been lucky so far with the amounts of honey I've given them?" asks Geoff.

"I know more now. Just one spoonful before their exams with this newly synthesised honey and they'll all fly through their tests. But only one spoonful each – and I've been meaning to tell you this, Geoff – make sure they don't have sports or break time any time soon after they've just eaten it," says Appleby.

"And why is that?" asks Rose now fuming.

"Because you will find them all jumping around the school, like you've just said, Rose. Which will certainly be of interest to the headmaster," says Appleby with a chuckle.

"Right! That's it you two! The headmaster will know about your little scheme first thing tomorrow. Have you got that! No more funny business from you two, especially if it involves the students," says Rose, storming towards the kitchen door.

"But Rose, the honey works so well, and after all – it is only honey! If you were to offer it to your students, as well, just think of the adulation we'll receive once the pupils get their good grades in the two most important subjects. We'll both be promoted to head of our departments which will mean pay rises, too. It's what we've both been aiming for if we were honest with each other," replies Geoff, still feeling drunk.

Rose still fumes but she looks to Geoff with a glimmer of interest in her eyes. It would impress Roger if she were to be made head of department. She ponders some more until she hears a knock, knock, on the farmhouse kitchen door.

To her horror, Roger then steps through into the farmhouse kitchen making Rose almost faint.

"Ah, hah! So this is where it's at, is it?" says Roger, scanning the three guilty looking culprits ahead of him.

"Roger! What on earth are you doing here?" replies Rose, still frozen with horror by the sight of him.

"Some kind of orgy going on, I see," says Roger ignoring Rose for the minute.

"There's no orgy going on, Roger," says Geoff, as calmly as he can but inside feeling as horrified as Rose looks.

"Let me be the judge of that," says Roger eying some of Rose's clothes still draped over the floor. "Rose is here. Geoff is here, and this must be the farmer, Russell Appleby, given that this is his farmhouse. Which can only mean one thing: trouble is afoot, and big trouble, I'm sure," says Roger, almost fuming.

"Take a seat, Roger. Calm down, will you," says Geoff.

"I will do no such thing," replies Roger. "Rose, I followed you. I had to, I'm afraid. You've been spending too many evenings away from me recently, stirring in your own juices, and I wanted to know why. And let me tell you the sight that greets me here now fills me only with dread and concern for you, Rose. You couldn't be in worse company. The headmaster will hear about this little get-together tomorrow morning, you can all be assured of that," adds Roger.

Appleby fumes as he approaches Roger. "Just who do you think you are? You, you little tyke! You barge into my home and start abusing the three of us for no apparent reason. You must get out of my kitchen right now!" replies Appleby, raising his arms ready to throw Roger out.

Roger quickly changes tack when he senses Appleby's aggressive intentions. He moves swiftly back towards the open kitchen door.

"Oh, Roger," replies Rose, feeling sorry for him, while also worrying about his safety.

Geoff still remains surprisingly calm. "What exactly is the headmaster going to hear tomorrow morning, Roger?" asks Geoff.

"He's going to hear that. . . He's going to hear that Rose is being led astray, once more, by Geoff and her newly found strange friend, the farmer, Russell Appleby. And that they are leading her into taking part in some kind of orgy," says Roger, now feeling quite afraid of the angry-looking Appleby towering above him.

"Get out of my house and off my farm, whoever you are! How can you have the nerve to barge into my kitchen and then be rude to me and my guests like this. Who are you, anyway?" fumes Appleby, ready to throw him outside.

Roger's already moving back out of the kitchen door. "The headmaster will hear about all of this, whatever is going on here. And something is going on here, I can sense it. I'm only thinking of you, Rose. You know that, don't you?" says Roger, as Appleby holds onto the handle of the open kitchen door before pushing Roger completely outside.

Roger eyes Rose with great concern from outside. "I'm only thinking of you, Rose," says Roger. He then gives Geoff an angry stare just before Appleby slams the kitchen door closed on him.

Inside the kitchen, Rose dashes towards the closed door.

"Wait, Roger!" says Rose, pulling open the door, then dashing out of the farmhouse into the darkness. "Wait for me," cries Rose, soon disappearing from sight.

Geoff closes the kitchen door calmly. "Well, that's it, Russell," he says. "Roger's sure to tell the headmaster about all of this, I'll lose my job and you – well, you'll lose your discovery. What were you thinking, going with Rose like that. I told you she was with Roger," adds Geoff.

"Don't blame me. It wasn't me – it was Rose. She was all over me as soon as she came round," says Appleby, making Geoff feel even more nauseous.

"Anyway, what's Roger going to say? His girlfriend has been seeing another man? This Roger doesn't know anything about what we're doing," adds Appleby confidently.

"Are you sure he doesn't know anything?" asks Geoff. "He's tenacious. He wants to protect Rose. He'll find out what he needs to know about us, one way or another," adds Geoff.

"We need to keep this Roger away from here, that's for sure but I trust Rose, somehow. I trust that Rose won't say anything more to Roger about our little venture," says Appleby. "She certainly doesn't want to get you into any more trouble."

"Yes, you're right, but Roger's not afraid to stir things up with the headmaster, which is what he will do, until he uncovers something. Rose will let something slip somehow, even if she doesn't mean to," adds Geoff. "I know her, you see."

"We need to keep Rose out of our equation from now on, if we can. It's for that reason that I haven't told you yet about another discovery I have made about this honey. It may look a bit suspicious if you give your students these refreshments before each exam. This Roger and the other teachers at your school might suspect something. So the good news is you may not need to give them the honey just before their exams. I've factored in a delay process that should make the effects of the honey last for about a week," says Appleby, excitedly. "You'll need to top them up for a second week, of course."

"So you mean the effects of the honey could last for the whole exam week? Meaning almost all off their exams will benefit?" asks Geoff excitedly.

"We can't let Rose and Roger derail us now. It was a great idea of yours, Geoff, what better way to market the product around here than to improve the exam grades of their sons or daughters. We'll make millions, eventually," says Appleby, wide-eyed.

Geoff is easily convinced by Appleby's business brain once more. He can only see a positive outcome to their little venture.

"Look, Geoff, I've got that presentation at the school on Friday," says Appleby, opening the kitchen door for Geoff. "The week after is their exam week so I will bring the honey along to the presentation," he adds.

"Mock exams," confirms Geoff.

"We must make sure the honey will work with the delay process involved," replies Appleby.

Geoff slopes out of the kitchen. "I'll bring the biscuits," says Geoff, disappearing into the darkness outside.

Chapter 11

That Friday afternoon, Russell Appleby drives slowly into the school car park. He carries a briefcase and several other bags towards the entrance of the school, where he finds Anthony Bright standing in the doorway to greet him with a smile on his face.

"Thank you for agreeing to give this talk, Mr Appleby. It's just what the children need – a diversion from their exams and tests next week," says Bright, shaking Appleby's hand.

"I hope it will be what you hoped for. A run-down of life on a local farm," replies Appleby.

"It'll be perfect provided you don't go into too much detail. They won't be able to concentrate too hard given the events coming up next week," replies Bright.

"Our little town of Honibridge is surrounded by farmland, so I'll give them an idea of what life around here used to be like for so many of its inhabitants," says Appleby, walking with the headmaster into the school.

An hour and a half later, applause fills the school hall after Appleby has concluded his little presentation. There are pictures of tractors and farm animals on the large board behind him.

"Now, it would be nice to hear from you if any of you have any questions about life on a farm. Have I managed to encourage any of you to go into farming when you leave school?" asks Appleby, looking towards the older students at the back of the hall.

"Where do those sheep come from, Mr Appleby?" asks Ernest Thompson from the back of the hall.

"Those that weren't born on our farm came from another sheep farm originally," replies Appleby.

"And what about the cows?" asks Sarah Jordan.

"They would have come from a cow farm originally," replies Appleby.

"So what about all those trees on your farm, Mr Appleby? Did they come from a tree farm?" asks Ben Andrews, making some of the younger pupils giggle.

"The trees grow from out of the ground," says Appleby quite seriously.

"Why do trees grow, Mr Appleby?" asks Thompson.

"Because they want to," replies Appleby.

"Why are some trees taller than other trees, Mr Appleby?" asks a younger, bespectacled student at the front of the hall.

"Because some trees are show offs," replies Appleby to more giggles from some of the pupils.

"Are you a show off, Mr Appleby?" asks Ernest Thompson.

Headmaster Bright feels it is time to bring the presentation to an end, so he strides forward from the back of the hall. "I think we all know the answer to that question judging by the expensive tweed jacket Mr Appleby wears comfortably on his shoulders," says Bright, shaking Appleby's hand and winking at him at the same time.

"Thank you for a most illuminating talk on the life of the farm, Mr Appleby. I certainly saw a glimmer of interest from some of the children and that's all that's needed for the time being," says Bright, addressing the school hall.

"Now, all of those Year Elevens with important mock exams next week, please step forward for some refreshments," says the headmaster, when he notices Appleby places some biscuits on the table at the front of the hall and then pour some blackcurrant juice into some plastic beakers.

As the older students arrive at the front of the hall, Ernest Thompson is the first to arrive and grab a biscuit. "Why do some of the students have refreshments while the younger ones do not, Mr Appleby?" asks Ernest quite sensibly.

"Because you older students deserve them more," replies Appleby.

"I don't think all of us older students deserve refreshments more than others, especially not Ernest Thompson," pipes up Sarah Jordan, smiling at Thompson.

"I think all of you Year Eleven pupils deserve refreshments after that quite enlightening talk by me," replies Appleby, passing around the beakers that contain the blackcurrant juice.

"If I was giving a presentation at a school, I wouldn't provide refreshments for the pupils," adds Sarah Jordan.

"Oh, why is that? It's what kind people would do. They would provide refreshments at the end of a presentation," replies Appleby.

"Why do we have kind people, Mr Appleby?" asks Ernest.

"We have kind people because they often provide refreshments to school pupils after presentations instead of giving them detention," replies Appleby.

"Yes, I can see why we should prefer kind people, Mr Appleby," replies Thompson, polishing off his blackcurrant juice, then helping himself to another biscuit.

"There seems to be a lot of kind people in this school then, Mr Appleby," says Andrews.

"Oh, why is that?" asks Appleby.

"Because we're always being given refreshments at school these days," adds Sarah Jordan.

"I'm glad to hear it, then," replies Appleby, looking nervously at the headmaster, who seems to be more interested in Appleby's SUV parked in the car park outside through the window, than his pupils in the school hall.

Ernest Thompson chomps into a provided biscuit, then joins the headmaster in observing the parked SUV.

A few minutes later, Geoff walks with Appleby towards his parked SUV in the car park, carrying some of Appleby's bags for him.

"Once they've drunk this honey, you are sure they won't all start jumping around the car park like a herd of kangaroos?" asks Geoff, worrying about their little venture more and more now that they have put it into practice.

"Of course they won't. As long as they have lessons now for a few hours and not sports or break time, the effects of the honey will be channelled into their minds and not their limbs," adds Appleby confidently. "The honey's been synthesised so now its effects will last until the mock exams are over," he adds.

Geoff looks at him questioningly. "I'm taking an awful risk you know. I'm as unsure about this whole venture as you seem confident about it."

"It's an imprecise science, Geoff, what we've discovered. It's new and this special honey will prove to be a breakthrough for us. I'm convinced of it," replies Appleby.

Geoff looks at him again with an even more furrowed and questioning brow. "Great," says Geoff.

"I'm just saying that risks need to be taken to advance our understanding of the world around us. We're in this together, remember," replies Appleby, before jumping into his SUV.

Geoff's far from convinced by everything that Appleby has just said to him and he's just about to tell

Appleby that their business venture should come to an end immediately, when he becomes temporarily blinded by a glint of sunlight that shines into his eyes from two lenses of a small pair of binoculars hidden from his sight.

Geoff squints from the reflected sunlight in his face at the same time that Max Heckton lowers his binoculars on the other side of the school car park, after observing Geoff and his friend in deep conversation. Heckton has been trying to lip-read their conversation but with no success: that is why Heckton bares his teeth in anger before growling with frustration.

Geoff is forced to ignore the glinting sunlight in his face from who knows where and concentrate on the dilemma in hand. "Russell, If you can keep away from us and this school as much as possible from now on, it would be appreciated," says Geoff.

"Do you mean keep away from Rose, too?" asks Appleby.

"I mean Rose; I mean me; I mean this school as well as this whole bee business now that the refreshments have been given. I certainly don't want to see you jumping through those fields again. You will be seen and caught if you do it again, I'm sure of it. You got that?" says Geoff forcefully.

Appleby smiles as he powers up his flashy SUV. "You know, Geoff, don't you, that Rose calls around for me," replies Appleby, making Geoff feel slightly sick. "But I know what you mean, Geoff. And I'll do my best for you," says Appleby, finally slamming the door shut on his large automobile.

Geoff tries to smile at him as he watches Appleby wheelspin his SUV out of the car park and onto the road outside. It is then that he feels the warm glow of the glinting sunlight over his face once more and this time he turns quickly to see Heckton in the distance, holding his binoculars and focusing on him from the school grounds to one side of the school.

Heckton quickly lowers his binoculars when he spies Geoff staring straight at him. "B's? B's?" says Heckton questioningly to himself. "There will be dodos landing in your back garden before any one of your students gets a B grade from your teaching, Wade," he adds to himself.

Yet there's something in the back of Heckton's mind that doesn't let this idea go and he returns to his first thought about the bits and pieces of the conversation that he managed to pick up between the two spied-on interlopers.

"Did they say bees, or B's?" asks Heckton, once again of himself.

Heckton gags suddenly when he feels his shirt collar pulled smartly upwards with a great thrust of strength from behind him. Heckton immediately knows who the culprit is before he turns to see the angry face of the headmaster, Anthony Bright, stare into his.

"Max, I've told you so many times about this before. I don't want you spying on other teachers. I am the headmaster and I will run this school as I see fit. I do not need any of my teachers trying to muscle in on my domain, especially not you, Max. Do you understand that? Start minding your own business and that is an order," booms Bright, angrily.

"But how else are we going to know what's going on right underneath our noses. I can tell you without question that there's something going on between Geoff Wade and that farmer, Appleby. I can smell it, and as you know from the desert, Anthony, I'm good at smelling out trouble. You wouldn't be here if I hadn't smelt that smell of trouble out there when I did," replies Heckton, releasing himself from Bright's mauling.

"Do you think so?" replies Bright, instantly suspecting that Heckton could be right about Wade but not letting on.

"Yes, very much so, in this instance. Have you ever known me to be wrong about my smells?" says Heckton, straightening his tie and knowing he's right.

Bright doesn't like Heckton but he instinctively knows Heckton is usually right about these smells he gets, because he has been right about them almost every time before. So he controls his composure as much as he can, given the circumstances, and lets up with the mauling of his geography teacher.

"If you continue to get involved with other teachers' business like this, don't be surprised if they start turning their attentions to your business, too," replies Bright.

"If you're not even going to talk to them about what they are up to, then it'll grow into a bigger problem for you and I'm sure I'll be seeing you out of a job before too long," says Heckton menacingly.

Bright fumes and as he does so, his right hand balls up into a fist ready to punch it into Heckton's face. However, on this occasion the headmaster manages to control his anger and resume his usual calm exterior, much to the disappointment of Heckton who was quite looking forward to the punch in the face.

Instead, Bright pushes Heckton away from the tree, forcing Heckton to lose his footing. Heckton falls but recovers quickly enough to turn the fall into a slip, so that he can walk back towards the school feeling some kind of satisfaction that he almost made the headmaster punch him in the face.

Bright shouts after him. "Remember, Max, if I need your help I'll ask for it!" Bright straightens his long black cloak and gathers his composure, only to find Geoff Wade stride towards him from the school.

Geoff had already been striding towards the fracas in the playing fields when it was in full flow, so by the time he reaches the headmaster, who seems visibly shaken to Geoff, Heckton has already disappeared back inside the school.

"Anthony, I saw that and it is the last time that sort of thing can happen to you. You need to report him right now; you are the headmaster, after all," says Geoff, not knowing that it was Bright who started this latest tussle between the two of them.

"I've told you: you leave Max for me to deal with," replies the headmaster.

"I've seen that you can't handle him. Do you want me to get involved? I will do it for your sake," asks Geoff.

"I've said that I can fight my own battles and that is what I must do, thank you very much," says Bright, now pondering over what Heckton has just told him as they walk back towards the school.

"But it seems to me that you can't fight your own battles," replies Geoff.

"Go away, Geoff, and this time I'm serious. If I hear more from you on this matter, I may well report you and not Heckton. And I suggest you stay well clear of Heckton as much as you can, for he is my concern now," says Bright.

"Well, this has to be the last time he gets away with that kind of behaviour. He's trouble and I've seen his threatening ways towards you before. If I see you two at loggerheads again, I will have to go over your head," replies Geoff.

"I appreciate your concern, Geoff, but you would do well to stay clear of Heckton and leave him to his own devices, as well as not bothering me with your constant concern for my welfare. Now that I have got you here, though, I've been talking with Roger," says Bright.

"Oh, yes?" asks Geoff feeling very worried.

"Roger was rambling on about something to me, you know, the way he does, incoherently as usual. He really should take some elocution lessons this summer if he can. I find it difficult to understand what he is talking about most of the time. The thing is he did mention your name," says Bright.

"In what connection?" asks Geoff.

"Well, that's the thing, Geoff. For the life of me, I can't remember. Perhaps he did tell me something or perhaps I couldn't understand what he was saying. . . The point is, there's no funny business going on is there? With you?" asks the headmaster.

"Funny business? " asks Geoff, appearing to look confused.

"Is there any funny business going on between you and that farmer, Russell Appleby?" asks Bright.

"You are not up to anything, are you? Have you any idea what Roger was talking about when he mentioned it to me? He did seem most annoyed by it all," adds Bright.

"I have no idea what Roger is talking about most of the time, like you, so I'm not sure what you're talking about or what Roger has been telling you, but I can guarantee you there's no funny business going on. I'm sure it's just one of Roger's worries getting hold of him again. He does worry a lot, you know. Rose has said he's a constant worrier," informs Geoff.

"Ah yes. Rose Daniels. Caring and understanding, Rose," replies Bright.

"It has been a difficult time for me, Anthony, there's no getting away from that fact, but I expect it's just Roger putting his oar into the soup yet again. He does nothing to make things easier for me, I can tell you that," says Geoff.

"Yes, I will have a word with Roger about that. He's always making accusations about you. He does seem to have it in for you. Perhaps he's jealous," replies Bright.

"I can't understand why. He's the one going out with Rose," says Geoff.

"Yes, of course, Geoff, and from what I hear you are turning around the fortunes of this year's exam students. I'm expecting good results from them this summer. If they get better grades than last year's Year Elevens, it could well mean a promotion for you. You do know that, don't you?" replies Bright.

"That's what I'm aiming for, headmaster," says Geoff.

"Good show, Geoff. Good show," says Bright, opening the door for Geoff to go back inside the school.

One evening, during the last week of Easter term and a few days after the mock exams, Geoff and Rose snog on the front seat of Geoff's battered, old second-hand car. They stop for breath.

"You, know, Rose, don't you, that I still love you?" says Geoff earnestly.

Rose guffaws into Geoff's face, much to his annoyance, making him become quite upset. "Don't be so silly, Geoff," she replies.

"I'm serious, Rose, and I think we should get back together," he says, plainly and honestly.

"Geoff, you're being ridiculous as usual," replies Rose.

"Am I, Rose? I've been hearing how keen you were to get me back to the school after my suspension," says Geoff.

"The headmaster told you this, I expect. Of course I was keen for you to come back to the school: you're a good teacher, when you want to be," she replies.

"He also told me that moving to a different school may be the best thing for me," says Geoff.

Now it is Rose's turn to feel upset. "Oh, I see. To be honest, I've just been wanting you to come back to our school, at least for the time being. If you want to go to another school, then fine – go!" replies Rose curtly.

Geoff's quite affected by her curt response and he knows that there surely must still be something left of their failed relationship. It fills him with a new confidence.

"I can tell that you don't mean that, Rose. You sounded quite upset when I suggested moving to a different school," he says.

"Yes, I do mean it, Geoff. You should just go. Get out of this old school and go – well, go anywhere. I don't care," she replies, looking tearful.

Geoff looks to her. "You are close to tears, Rose," he says.

"No, I'm not," she replies, knowing she must look quite upset to Geoff. Rose looks out of her side window into the darkness to try to hide her face from him.

"You, know, Rose, I hate Appleby in some ways for going with you, but somehow he might just be turning things around for me in other ways," says Geoff, changing tack.

Rose wants to avoid the topic of Appleby's honey as much as she can. "That's good, Geoff, I've noticed an improvement in you, too," she replies.

"It's not just this honey that Appleby's developed. I mean the honey's helped, but I think it has sort of inspired me to help my pupils as best as I can and to really improve their grades, regardless of whether we use the honey or not. It's a risk I'm taking, using the honey, but I still want to take that risk for the sake of the students. Has it inspired you, too?" asks Geoff.

"I'm afraid you shouldn't have mentioned the honey to me. It was exactly the wrong thing to talk about if you were hoping we would get back together some day. Exactly the wrong thing to talk about – well done, Geoff! I knew you would spoil our chances somehow. You know I don't agree with any of this honey business. If someone finds out about all of this, you'll be out of a job, then where's your pay rise you've been hoping for?" replies Rose.

"If someone finds out about all of this, we'll both be out of a job," says Geoff.

"How dare you threaten me!" replies Rose.

"I'm just trying to make sure that you keep our little venture well away from Roger's grasping hands. If Roger finds out about this, then all is lost and I'm afraid I will have to mention your name somewhere along the line," says Geoff.

"I've told you I won't tell him anything but you know Roger's got high standards: he knows the difference between right and wrong and I respect him for that. In some ways, I'm keeping our little secret from him so that I don't have to drag him down to our level," replies Rose, while she looks towards the vulnerable-looking and emotionally unstable Geoff sitting next to her.

"Do you really need this pay rise so badly?" adds Rose, already knowing the answer.

"It is more than that, as I've just been trying to tell you. Improving the students' grades is something I've found that, somewhere deep down, I want to do. I've never realised it before until Appleby got involved. I thought I went into teaching for– well, I don't know why I went into teaching, but from what I've been hearing, all reports point towards a good crop of mock-exam results, probably as the result of that specially bred honey this time, but it has helped me realise that

that is what I am a teacher for. Besides, I always need a pay rise that badly," says Geoff, as he looks out of the front windscreen into the darkness, while Rose, sitting next to him, sighs a deep sigh.

Chapter 12

It is near to the end of April and the sun shines brightly and warmly over Honibridge Modern. Geoff strides purposefully and energetically into the school, feeling confident and excited about his prospects for the forthcoming summer term.

He forcefully pushes open the door to the staffroom, then strides into the room making all the other, less eager-feeling teachers look at him with wonder. He immediately sets his eyes on Rose, sitting on the far side of the staffroom talking with what must be a new teacher.

Geoff strides through the milling teachers around him, eager to find out exactly who Rose is in deep conversation with. Geoff's about to introduce himself to the short, round, yet sharply dressed new teacher, Arthur Crook, when the headmaster, Anthony Bright, begins to speak from his raised pulpit to one side and addresses his congregation.

"Welcome. . ." says Bright just before his attention is stunningly grabbed by the staffroom door opening quietly and smoothly ahead of him to reveal a tall, elegant and attractive-looking woman in her mid-twenties who glides effortlessly into the room.

Bright is forced to stay silent for a moment, because everyone else immediately turns their heads to look at the attractive creature that has just swanned into the staffroom and grabbed everyone's attention.

Susan Chalmers, twenty-six years of age, smiles as she tosses her long blonde hair from one side to the other and looks for somewhere to perch herself. Rose holds her hand over her mouth, as if she's almost about to wretch. She's instantly sickened by this woman's attractiveness and certain of the trouble she will cause amongst her fellow teachers.

Geoff is no different to all the other teachers in the room, because when he sees her he doesn't take his eyes off her as she glides towards an empty chair. He's completely unaware that the papers he holds slide, one by one, onto the floor in front of him while he stares, open-mouthed, towards the glamorous-looking, model-type woman who has just taken centre stage in the Honibridge Modern staffroom.

Susan Chalmers always loves the attention she attracts wherever she goes, so she is not surprised to find the staffroom in a state of hush because of her. She finally takes a seat next to Rose on the other side of Geoff. This is when Geoff finally notices Rose look at him angrily, which hastily breaks the spell the beauty has held over him up to this point.

Geoff soon comes right back to his senses when Max Heckton strides through the doorway into the staff room, unusually late. Heckton could hear a pin drop if one was dropped right now, so he makes his way towards an empty chair on the other side of the room, happily ignorant, for the time being, of the reason why the staff room is as quiet as it is.

As he walks towards an empty chair, Heckton soon notices Geoff straight ahead of him, so he gives him an aggressive, teeth-bared grin just before he slips and slides on some of Geoff's dropped papers, causing Heckton to fall to the floor.

Rose has to stifle a cheer when she finds Heckton looking angrily up at her from the floor and this does nothing for Heckton's already angry and upset morning. Heckton fumes a deep, red colour when he gets to his feet.

He immediately puts his head to Geoff's head and bares his teeth angrily, once more, despite the headmaster staring at him, open-mouthed. Geoff doesn't react, for this reason, so he sits there passively until Heckton has moved his head away and taken a seat nearby.

Heckton then scans the two new teachers quickly before taking a back seat in proceedings when he notices the headmaster stare at him angrily. It is at this point that Geoff notices Susan Chalmers now looking towards the angry, red-faced Heckton and to Geoff's consternation she seemingly gets a hot flush from

Heckton's recent aggressive antics. As Susan's face reddens too, to match Heckton's, it is Geoff's turn to now feel nauseous. Surely this gorgeous woman can't find this very unpleasant individual attractive, can she, he ponders.

The headmaster remains tight lipped until Heckton's angry little display in the middle of the staff room has quite finished. Headmaster Bright then quickly snaps back into his train of thought and resumes his address.

"Welcome, fellow teachers and I'm glad to see you all back again. I hope you all had a relaxing Easter holiday and are refreshed and ready for the summer exam term. Let's start with some good news for the English and Maths departments, Year Eleven's mocks were all passed with flying colours. And when I say all, I do remarkably mean all, for there was not one failure amongst them. I know what you're going to say and yes, I did check through some of the papers myself, just to be sure, but I'm glad to say I could not find any errors in our marking system, so well done to all of you who work in those departments. I hope to hear similar results from the other subject departments at the end of the summer.

"Now, we have some more good news for you. We have two new members of staff joining us – I expect you have already noticed – Miss Susan Chalmers will be joining our Geography Department until the end of the year, while Mr Arthur Crook will be joining our overstretched Maths Department for as long as he's needed. So let us give a round of applause for our new members of staff, as well as all the good work that has been done in the Maths and English Departments over the year," says Bright, as some kind of applause begins to ring around the staffroom, leaving Arthur Crook to smile meekly from his chair in the corner and Susan Chalmers to smile a winning smile and then almost bow towards the clapping teachers until the applause finally subsides.

"Now, as you will probably have heard, Mr Philpott's social-mobility scooter was stolen yet again while he attended a recent council meeting. This means he is currently house-bound until he recovers the stolen scooter or gets a replacement. So you will find an envelope being passed around the room and we would be grateful for any contributions you could make towards helping our very favourite woodwork teacher, Mitchell Philpott, to reclaim his scooter and return to the school as soon as possible," adds Bright.

Geoff guffaws when he hears this. He has absolutely no intention of giving any money whatsoever to a teacher that he has disliked since the day they first met. The envelope finally reaches him. He shakes the contents of the envelope. He judges there to be a few loose coins rattling around at the bottom of it, which causes him to have a change of heart.

Geoff feels generous for once. He drops a pound coin into the envelope. "What's this going to buy him, a new padlock for his scooter?" says Geoff to no one in particular, making Rose roll her eyes and forcing her to give a five-pound donation to Philpott's cause.

The headmaster soon wraps up his sermon, allowing the other teachers to swarm around him for advice and guidance. Geoff leaves Rose in the staffroom and walks through the school corridor towards his first class of the new term.

He doesn't quite reach his first class because Max Heckton approaches him from the other direction, just before he reaches his classroom. Heckton then guides Geoff towards the wall of the corridor without actually touching him.

"You and Appleby. What's going on with you and that farmer, Appleby?" says Heckton. "I'm going to be watching you like a hawk this term, Wade. I heard you talk with him last term and it's been playing on my mind ever since. What were you two really talking about in the car park? Something's going on and I'm going to find out what it is," threatens Heckton before he snorts and walks rudely away.

"Thanks, Heckton, for that. Don't expect me to be watching you in the same way, will you?" says Geoff towards the back of Heckton's tweed jacket. Geoff soon regains his composure, determined not to let Heckton spoil his first day of term. He walks towards his classroom just as Susan Chalmers sweeps around the corner and glides towards him from the opposite direction.

Geoff is just about to introduce himself when Susan calls out after Heckton at the far end of the corridor, so she picks up her step to catch up with him leaving Geoff to stand alone and watch her disappear around the corner.

Geoff still can't believe that this gorgeous woman has any interest in Heckton. He assumes it must be a purely professional reason because they will be working in the same department, so he dismisses them out of his mind, opens the door to his classroom, and walks inside.

Around the corner of the corridor, Susan finally catches up with her appointed Geography mentor, Max Heckton.

"Mr Heckton! Mr Heckton," says Susan, out of breath when she finally reaches him.

"What do you want?" replies Heckton rudely.

"I'm new at this school, Mr Heckton. My name is Susan Chalmers – the one the headmaster just introduced in the staff room – and I was wondering if you could show me around, if you have the time, of course. We're going to be working in the same department, did you know that, Mr Heckton?" says Susan, really trying to connect with him.

"I have no time for you now," says Heckton curtly. "Get lost," he adds, before walking swiftly away from her.

Susan leans against the corridor wall. She's never been spoken to so rudely before: it is a revelation to her and she thinks she quite likes it. Susan has another hot flush as she turns her head towards Heckton, just before he disappears inside a classroom. She looks longingly towards this excitingly dismissive teacher that she has just spoken to for the first time.

One evening, later that week, Geoff drives his spluttering old car through the darkness along a lane then turns onto the gravel driveway of Russell Appleby's farmhouse. He drives up the gravel driveway towards the lighted farmhouse, then parks up just in front of the kitchen window. He turns the key in the ignition to turn the engine off but as usual, the car splutters on and refuses to switch off. He gets out of the car then slams its door closed. The car immediately turns itself off and sits quietly on the gravel.

Geoff is about to knock on the kitchen door when he hears noises from the fields behind him. He's about to knock again but Geoff finds the noises from the field quite insistent, so he leaves the kitchen door alone and creeps through the shrubbery into the nearest field to the farmhouse to find out where the noises come from.

The noises soon become more distinct and Geoff can tell that they are the noises of some very deeply humming bees. Why they should be humming so loudly at this hour in the darkness Geoff does not know, but he does know his way to Appleby's bee hives from here, so he sets off through the darkness towards them to investigate.

As Geoff gets closer to the bee hives, he's troubled by the deep humming sounds of the bees: they have never sounded this loud to him before. He becomes quite wary of making his way onwards and his suspicions soon become heightened when he notices two moving figures in the darkness under the moonlight, near to the bee hives just ahead of him.

"Russell? Is that you, Russell?" whispers Geoff trying not to disturb the humming bees as much as possible.

There's no reply from the two mysterious figures ahead of him and Geoff is just about to hide in the nearby shrubbery, when he notices the two figures take flight and run away into the darkness in the opposite direction.

Geoff is pleased that he's managed to scare away the interlopers so easily but he wonders why they were there. Surely Appleby would have replied if one of them had been him. Then two bright headlights of an SUV approach slowly through a distant field towards him. Geoff doesn't want to run into any more strangers, so this time he does hide in the shrubbery until he knows more about the inhabitants of the approaching car.

He can hear the deeply humming bees not far away in their hives and he wonders what had been going on there before he arrived. The SUV finally stops just ahead of him beaming its bright light over the bee hives. Someone steps out from the driver's door as Geoff tenses in the shrubbery. Appleby's shiny forehead soon appears in front of the bright lights of the SUV making Geoff finally breathe out with relief. He still stays hidden for the immediate moment.

"Russell? Is that you?" asks Geoff.

"Geoff? What are you doing here?" replies Appleby quite casually, given the circumstances.

Geoff appears from out of the shrubbery. "I've been keeping out of your way recently because– well, there are those that want to expose out little venture and get me into trouble, but that honey that we gave the kids for their mocks – it worked wonders. I expect you already know so I just came round to tell you, in case you'd forgotten that we're going to need a new supply of the stuff for their real exams," says Geoff.

"Of course, Geoff – in time," replies Appleby distractedly, with his mind on other things. "Couldn't you have come round a bit earlier to tell me this? It scares me to find you creeping around in the darkness on my farm, you know," replies Appleby.

Their conversation is cut short because they can both hear the sound of another car drive slowly up the gravel driveway near to the farmhouse behind them. "Damn. They're early," says Appleby.

"Who's early? What's going on, Russell?" asks Geoff. "Who were those two people running away into that field just now? What were they doing here?" adds Geoff.

"What two people? In what field?" asks Appleby, getting quite concerned.

Geoff does not reply because he can see Appleby's now fully occupied by the inhabitants of the large car that has just parked up in the farmhouse driveway.

"Who is it, Russell?" asks Geoff as they creep through the darkness towards the driveway.

"Geoff, you shouldn't be here. This is no place for you now," replies Appleby.

"Why ever not?" asks Geoff.

Appleby grabs hold of Geoff's arm. "Geoff, if you have to stay here, stay well hidden. Leave this to me," replies Appleby, when they approach the two large headlights of the car that beam towards them through the trees.

Appleby quickly pushes Geoff to the ground to keep him out of sight of the beaming headlights and Geoff is in no mood to question Appleby's actions, so he stays on the ground and well out of the way of the parked car and its hidden inhabitants.

After a short while, two burly-looking men get out of the parked car and stand in front of the beaming headlamps that make them appear even more burly and dangerous than they first appeared.

"Geoff, whatever you do, do not show yourself," whispers Appleby into the darkness. "They're only expecting to meet with me, so that's the way we'll keep it," adds Appleby.

Once Appleby is sure that Geoff remains out of sight, he approaches the two sinister-looking men, each gripping a holdall, shadowed against the bright headlamps of their car.

Appleby can hear the deep humming coming from the inside of each of the holdalls and it thrills him with delight, although he tries to hide it as best he can from the two unfriendly-looking men standing in front of him.

"You have the merchandise I requested?" asks Appleby.

"You have the money?" asks one of the men gruffly.

Appleby takes out two thick wads of crisp and packaged bank notes from the inside pocket of his tweed jacket, then approaches the two men apprehensively.

One of the men slowly puts on a pair of thick gloves, then unzips his holdall, keeping it closed until Appleby gets close enough to peek inside to observe the contents.

Appleby peeks inside the bag, then quickly pulls back when the humming from inside the holdall scares him a little. Appleby soon regains his composure to take another look.

"There's one in each bag?" asks Appleby.

The two men both nod slowly in answer. Appleby then throws the two wads of money down onto the ground in front of one of the mysterious men.

The man grabs hold of the wads of notes, checks the money is all there, then nods to his comrade, whereupon the two men put the deeply humming holdalls slowly and gently onto the ground and then walk back towards their car.

"I hope I don't see either of you here again. If I do, there will be trouble," says Appleby.

"If there's anything wrong with this money, then you'll be the one in trouble, my friend," replies one of the men in a foreign accent before he and his colleague jump back inside the car, slamming the doors closed.

Appleby puts on his thick pair of gloves, then grabs hold of the two holdalls while he watches the men's large car reverse slowly out over the gravel and drive away.

Appleby breathes out with a sigh of relief when the men's car disappears from sight. He then hurriedly carries the loudly humming contents of the holdalls into the trees behind the farmhouse.

He's shocked when he finds Geoff appear out of the bushes because he's almost forgotten about him in all the excitement.

"You weren't here tonight, Geoff – you got that?" says Appleby, carrying both holdalls into the darkness towards his precious bee hives in the fields, not far away. Geoff says nothing but remains curious about the contents of the two holdalls, so he follows Appleby into the darkness.

They soon approach two, new, tall bee hives silhouetted under a bright moon in a field not too far from the other bee hives. Appleby carefully places the two humming holdalls on the ground near to the two empty bee hives, then wipes his brow.

Appleby takes no time in fumbling around underneath one of the bee hives until he pulls out a netted head-protector that he hastily pulls over his head. He then unzips one of the holdalls, still barely remembering that Geoff is standing near him, and pulls out one of the deeply humming but drowsy-looking, incredibly large bees.

"My oh my, Appleby, what have you got there?" asks Geoff, taking several cautious steps backwards.

"This bee is even bigger than I expected," replies Appleby.

"Is that even a bee? It looks too big to be a bee. You are crazy, Russell, to be messing around with these things. One sting from one of those beauties and you won't be making any more honey ever again," says Geoff.

"These are two of the biggest Uruguayan queen bees I've ever seen, Geoff – worth every penny I've spent on them. With the bumble bees from my other hives, we'll soon produce enough of my special honey to satisfy all of my customers' needs," says Appleby, carefully placing the queen bee inside one of the newly built hives.

"Come back nearer to your exams and I'll have all that precious honey your students will need and then some, Geoff," replies Appleby, far too engrossed with his newly acquired merchandise to give Geoff another thought.

Now that Geoff has seen what Appleby has in his two holdalls, he's more than happy to slope away as quickly as he can before the large, drowsy queen bees wake up and give them both a fright. He's not quite sure whether Appleby knows what he is doing with these monster bees but Appleby has produced the goods before, so he decides to trust him and leave him to his business.

It seems to Geoff that there will be a plentiful supply of the honey nearer to exam time, so he bounds back through the darkness toward his battered old car, parked in the farmhouse driveway, and hopes that Appleby can muddle his way through whatever he has planned until the summer.

Chapter 13

Geoff chats with Rose in the school playground during lunch break the next day. For the moment he keeps last night's activities at Appleby's farmhouse to himself.

Rose is the first to notice Max Heckton stride towards them both with a stern-looking scowl all over his face. It's not long before Geoff notices him, too.

Heckton has no time for pleasantries, as usual. He immediately wades in as rudely as always when he reaches them.

"I know your little game, Wade. I'm onto you," says Heckton, knowing all too well that Rose must be aware of Geoff's little venture too.

"Go away, Heckton," replies Geoff, not at all pleased to see Heckton today.

"I saw you at Appleby's farmhouse last night with those bees, Geoff," says Heckton, causing Geoff's face to drop with horror.

Geoff can't quite believe Heckton knows about their little venture and he wonders how he ever found out about Appleby. It makes Geoff go quite white with worry, which Rose notices all too quickly.

"It was you at Appleby's place last night?" asks Geoff, remembering the two hooded figures disappearing into the darkness just before the two mysterious men arrived with the bees.

Heckton nods his head with satisfaction at making Geoff's face go so white but his smile soon turns to a frown when he notices Susan Chalmers glide through the playground towards them, with only one thing on her mind: Max Heckton.

Chalmers ignores Geoff and Rose and approaches Heckton with purpose. She stands uncomfortably close to him so that she can almost whisper into his ear.

"Max, do you have a free moment?" she asks charmingly.

"What do you want?" replies Heckton rudely, whilst baring his teeth.

"Year Eight? Human Geography?" says Chalmers, surprised that Max can't remember saying he would explain where they are with the subject.

"Oh yes," says Heckton, staring at Geoff all the while and still baring his teeth.

"You know, Max, I don't like the way you approach Geoff whenever you do. It's not the way to approach any teacher at this school and I may have to say something to the headmaster about it if you continue to behave like this," replies Rose, trying to defend Geoff.

Heckton says nothing in reply. He remains threateningly close to Geoff, completely ignoring what

Rose has just said to him. Geoff says nothing either, leaving Heckton to quickly get bored but remain as angry as ever.

Heckton finally looks to Susan for the first time and as much as he doesn't want to, he walks back towards the school with Susan as close to him as she can possibly get.

Susan puts her arm through Heckton's as they walk towards the school door. As they approach the school, she suddenly bursts out with laughter for no apparent reason while Heckton keeps a steely stern face. Susan then opens the door and they both disappear inside the school.

"I can't see that little relationship ever taking off, can you, Geoff?" says Rose.

"Those two in a relationship? Impossible," replies Geoff.

Roger Little steers his deep-throbbing Porsche into the bowls club later that evening, with Rose sitting next to him. There has been a silence and an uneasiness between the two of them for the whole journey. Roger finally can't hold his secret in any longer and he bursts forth with his recent discovery.

"I know what you and Geoff have been up to at Russell Appleby's place," bursts out Roger.

"Geoff's made a new friend, that's all," says Rose, immediately sensing that Roger knows something that he shouldn't.

"Don't play the innocent with me. Those refreshments you've been providing for the students – it's not just blackcurrant juice in those beakers is it?" says Roger.

"I don't know what you're talking about, Roger. The students are on a high that's all. They're working hard and getting the results they deserve," replies Rose.

Roger guffaws loudly. "You're telling me they're on a high and you're the ones making them so. Or I'm hoping against hope that it is only Geoff providing these refreshments and that you had the sense not to get involved," says Roger, parking his car on the gravel driveway of the bowls club, just outside the front door.

"Geoff's just turned things around, that's all. Just like I expected him to," replies Rose.

"Not just Geoff though, is it? You're getting better results from your students as well and it all seems to have happened since you first met with this farmer Russell Appleby," says Roger.

Rose has tears in her eyes which Roger quickly notices. "Geoff's got his act together and so have I," she states. "You can't try and spoil things for us now, Roger. You simply can't." Rose looks him straight in the eyes.

"Rules are rules, Rose," says Roger, smugly.

"But we haven't broken any rules," replies Rose angrily.

"Rose, I was at Appleby's place last night with Heckton. We both saw those bee hives and we found some jars of honey in a shed nearby that looked remarkably like the ones I've been seeing in your school bag recently," says Roger. "I could have expected you to start providing refreshments for the pupils, but Geoff? Geoff would never start providing refreshments without reason or out of the kindness of his heart," adds Roger.

"You were with Heckton last night? You are on Heckton's side now?" says Rose angrily. "Well, that's it! That is the final straw. What were you doing with him?"

"We were both doing a spot of snooping for the headmaster," says Roger.

Rose's heart sinks. If the headmaster is on their side then she and Geoff have no chance. "And you jump to anything the headmaster asks you to do?" replies Rose.

"I certainly think I do, Rose, He is the headmaster, after all," says Roger.

Rose sighs a deep sigh just as Malcolm Purdy opens the door of the bowls club to see who has just arrived in the car park. Rose opens her car door, keen to stop her conversation with Roger as soon as she can.

She's just about to step out of the car when she notices Malcolm Purdy wearing one of the ladies bowls players' outfits, complete with pleated skirt, approaching their car. Rose quickly closes her car door again, not quite sure what to do.

"Have you seen Malcolm?" asks Rose.

Roger turns to look at Malcolm out of his rear window as Purdy takes a gulp from his pint of beer while, with his other hand, pointing his gold-ring-covered fingers skyward. Rose feels forced to open her door again and greet him, no matter how she is feeling.

"Malcolm, I was wondering where you were," says Rose getting out of the car.

"Didn't I see you both the last time you were here? Probably had business to attend to, I expect. The bowls club does not run itself, unfortunately," replies Purdy, holding the car door open for Rose to get out.

"Just running in the ladies outfit I see, Malcolm?" says Roger with a smirk on his face, as he reluctantly gets out of his car on the other side.

"Much more comfortable than the men's outfit, Roger, especially when you're kneeling to bowl. Perhaps you would like to try one on, too? They've just arrived," asks Purdy.

"I'm not sure that would be quite my thing, Malcolm. I'm only one of your minions. I'll leave you to try them out for size," replies Roger, slamming his car door closed as he looks to Rose.

"You're not one of those narrow-minded types are you, Roger?" replies Purdy.

"Certainly not," replies Roger while they all walk into the bowls club together.

"Good, because I need a new dress for the summer ball and I am hoping you'll be able to come with me to search for one," replies Purdy.

At first Roger thinks Malcolm is joking, so he chuckles heartily because there is nothing in Purdy's very masculine-shaped body to suggest he would look good in a dress and judging by his appearance in the ladies outfit he now wears, they would have a very hard job finding a single dress to suit him.

But as Roger looks to Malcolm, he can find no hint of a smile on Malcolm's face so he assumes he must be serious.

"I'm afraid I can't tomorrow, Malcolm: it's a school day," says Roger, feeling relieved.

"How about Saturday then, Roger? There's still some time before the summer ball and I was hoping you could try on some dresses with me. You may look quite fetching in one, perhaps?" replies Purdy.

"Ahh, I can't," says Roger unthinkingly.

"We can't Malcolm, not on Saturday," says Rose. "Roger's got one of his behaviour-management courses to attend," she adds, while Roger pulls at his shirt collar to try and cool himself down.

"That is a shame. Perhaps another time, then," says Purdy, looking sternly at Roger, still determined to take him shopping for dresses whenever he can.

"Yes, perhaps," replies Roger.

Purdy leads Roger and Rose into the bowls club to find it empty because they are early and the first ones there. Purdy orders a couple of drinks for them while he polishes off his pint of beer. Roger's feeling far from comfortable standing next to Purdy wearing one of the ladies bowls outfits and despite looking forward to playing bowls, he feels he can't stay at the club any longer, so when he takes hold of his whisky Roger immediately spills it all over the floor.

"You know, Rose, you know that behaviour management course you talked of. I had almost completely forgotten about it and as you can imagine there's a lot I need to prepare for it before Saturday. I'm sorry about this, Malcolm, but we need to leave straight away because I have some work to do for it," says Roger, tugging at Rose to try and pull her towards the swinging front door.

"But you've both just arrived. Surely you can squeeze in at least one game," replies Purdy.

"No time, now. No time at all. Behaviour management I find to be a sticky subject," replies Roger, successfully pulling Rose towards the door.

"I'm sorry Malcolm, Roger's right. School these days. . . becoming very hectic. We're nearing the end of the school year, too," replies Rose, as they both almost skip towards the door.

"You both need to keep up the practice, you know. As long as you make up for this missed session!" shouts Purdy towards an already empty, swinging-closed door.

Outside Roger fumbles around in his pocket for the keys to his gleaming red Porsche parked outside. It puts all of the other cars in the car park to shame and Roger knows it.

"He would have been on about his shopping for dresses all night until he had cornered me for a date," replies Roger. "I know of another bowls club not too far away, smaller and not so competitive, less high-octane, if you know what I mean. Malcolm can get so intense he scares me," says Roger to an understanding and silently agreeing Rose as she climbs into the passenger seat.

Roger starts his loudly throbbing sports car, then wheelspins his Porsche out of the bowls club as quickly as he can.

Several weeks later, outside Honibridge Modern a robin flutters towards the window of the school hall one fine and warm, late-spring evening. The robin can see a host of people seated around a large table in the centre of the school hall, all involved in a heated debate. It has soon seen enough. The robin flutters its wings and flies away.

Inside the school hall it is the headmaster, Anthony Bright, who sits at the head of the table trying to regain some order to proceedings after an overheated parent-teacher meeting.

There are five teachers and a similar number of parents all seated around the large table in the centre of the room and they are all trying to get their voices heard. For most of the meeting, it is the parents' voices that are winning.

Sharon Thistle, mother of Archibald Thistle, a Year Eleven pupil, looks very concerned indeed and it is she who almost bursts into tears first. It requires Anthony Bright to step in and restore order.

"Order, order. . . Let's all calm down now, shall we? We will never get to the root of this discussion if we continue to all shout out at the same time," says Bright authoritatively and firmly, immediately bringing the overheated parents to order. "I've tried and tried to convince you all that what you have been hearing on the grapevine is merely rumours but it does not seem to be sinking in.

"If there were any truth to these rumours, then I would be sitting here telling you about them in detail and what I intended to do about them. I can assure you that Mr Wade, Miss Daniels and Mr Little have all been working extremely hard this year trying to bring your pupils up to the required standard and I have only praise for all three of them for improving so many of their grades in the mock exams. In addition to this, many of the students have excelled even beyond that which has been expected of them. This includes some children of parents who sit around this table."

"Yes, well, that's just the point – why have they improved so greatly? And in maths, too, of all subjects. My wife and I were never any good at maths at school yet now my son's even talking about taking maths at A' level. I don't know where these rumours started," says Chris Bagshott, the father of Lincoln Bagshott, another Year Eleven student, as he looks directly at the headmaster, who now has now doubt at all about where these rumours must have started, when he glances towards Max Heckton to one side of the table.

"But if there is some truth to them, then – like this other lady said here – it could ruin our children's futures if you fill their minds with ideas above their station in life," adds Bagshott to loud mumbling agreement from the other parents seated around the table, leaving the teachers, Geoff, Rose and Roger, not being amongst them, to roll their eyes with annoyance regarding the whole subject.

"Exactly," adds Martin Summers, father of Bethany Summers, another pupil in Year Eleven. "And why are the three culprits of these rumours not here to answer for themselves?" he adds. "I say sack the three of them. Sack all three of them, then the rumours will stop and my son can take his exams with no worries hanging over the results. I say we get a petition going and get as many parents to sign it as possible, so that we can rid our school of these three troublesome teachers before the end of the school year," adds Bagshott to hearty applause from all the other gathered parents.

Anthony Bright fumes and goes a bright red colour when he hears these threats from the parents. He snaps the already snapped pencil that he holds in half again.

"We cannot sack three teachers based on rumours," Bright responds "And what exactly are these rumours that you have heard? You all seem to be angry because your children are getting better exam results than you did when you were at school. Is that the real reason for your anger?"

The parents seated around the table go quiet for a moment but Bright can tell that they will not back down from their threats and will not be happy until they have got their pound of flesh. All eyes from the teachers and the parents now focus on the headmaster, who remains silent for a good long while.

Not even the teachers have any idea what to expect from their headmaster now and it makes everyone around the table feel quite nervous. Bright still does not say anything but he does quickly glance his eyes towards Max Heckton sitting at the other end of the table. Once he has Heckton's attention, he glances his eyes towards Chris Bagshott sitting opposite Heckton.

Heckton rapidly picks up on the message Bright is sending him. His eyes quickly glance over Bagshott, then return to the headmaster and he gives a very faint nod towards him that no one else notices, just to confirm he has understood Bright's intentions.

Heckton bares his teeth at Bagshott, then points his pencil towards the slightly taken-aback parent, making Bagshott sit back in his chair and feel quite frightened. Eventually Bagshott becomes angry while he waits for the headmaster to speak, so he speaks first.

"Let's take a vote on it. All those in favour of sacking the three teachers caught up in these rumours should raise their hands now," says Bagshott. "What we can achieve, even based on rumours, should mean that these three guilty teachers will have to find different schools to teach in from next term."

Bright now immediately cuts in. "Now, let's not be hasty here. There's no proof that these teachers have been involved in any activity that warrants any sackings. Let us calmly consider the options available to us that do not involve such drastic action. These three teachers are valued staff," replies the headmaster.

"All those in favour of sacking the three teachers involved in these rumours raise your hands now," says Bagshott loudly and forcefully, as he looks towards Heckton with defiance.

All of the parents quickly raise their hands, as do one or two of the teachers, including Heckton himself. The teachers soon put their hands down when Bright stares back at them.

"That's a majority even just around this table, Mr Bright," says Bagshott with satisfaction.

"I can't believe your attitude towards my teachers. These three teachers have been working very hard all year on your behalf and this is how you treat them? You do realise that our Year Eleven mock exam results outperformed all of the other schools' exam results in the area?" replies Bright, trying to defend his teachers.

"The decision has been made and voted on. If you do not sack these three teachers before the end of the school year then– well, I'm not sure what we'll do, but we will cause problems for you until you do," adds Sharon Thistle in support of Bagshott.

"Our children's final exam results are in jeopardy if these three teachers remain at this school during their summer exams. We will get the press involved if you do not act swiftly, Mr Bright," says Bagshott, sensing victory.

"You're all behaving completely irrationally," Bright states. "Do you know how difficult it is to get new teachers into a school? And these three teachers are working wonders. I can't understand your attitude. I've a good mind to get replacement parents for our next parent-teacher meeting."

"You just try. You just try!" replies Bagshott, getting angrily to his feet.

Bright gets up angrily from his seat too and he strides over to the side of the hall to refill a glass with water from a jug on a table by the side of the room. As he does so, he turns his back on all the teachers and parents seated around the table behind him, to try and think of a way out of this awkward situation.

The headmaster gulps down the glass of water then, shortly after, turns to face the troublesome table ahead of him. He quickly glances towards Heckton again to make sure he knows what he has to do later, leaving Bagshott and the other parents to sit back in their seats and look smugly back towards him.

The rest of the meeting remains as calm as the headmaster can keep it until fifteen minutes later the parent-teacher meeting is dissolved. The teachers especially cannot wait to get out of the hall. It is left to the headmaster to say goodbye to all of the parents and thank them for attending, while keeping Bagshott in conversation as much as possible until all of the other parents have left the hall.

Bright then escorts Bagshott out of the hall and into the early darkness of the evening, where they walk towards their cars parked in the car park. Bright soon arrives at his car leaving Bagshott to walk towards the tree-lined corner of the car park where he has parked his car.

"Good night, Mr Bagshott," says the headmaster.

"By the end of the summer term, headmaster – do you understand?" replies Bagshott.

Bright is already inside his car and does not hear Bagshott's final words but he does slam his door closed angrily because he did faintly hear Bagshott say something or other.

Chris Bagshott reaches his car, parked in the corner of the car park, and fumbles around in his pocket for his car keys feeling quite good about himself after expressing himself so well in the school hall moments earlier.

It is not something that he has ever done before, speaking up for himself so forcefully, and he has done it in the first parent-teacher meeting that he has ever attended, so it fills him with a new confidence that makes him determined to attend many more such meetings in the future, so that he can once again speak up for the downtrodden parents who, he believes, rarely have a say in how their children's schooling progresses.

Chris Bagshott opens the door to his car but he feels nervous for some reason. It is quite dark but there is a dim glimmer from a light on the other side of the car park that shines over his car just enough for him to see what he is doing.

However, it doesn't take long for Bagshott to realise that there is someone standing just behind him. Bagshott turns to see who it is and his face immediately turns white with horror. The car door slams closed behind him when Heckton pins Bagshott against the side of the car.

Bagshott's eyes widen with fright when Heckton's ugly, toothy face hisses into his. He somehow knows what to expect from Heckton, so he just slides down against the car door, hoping against hope that Heckton will do no more to him than just frighten him but it soon turns out that Bagshott will not be so lucky tonight.

Anthony Bright has already lowered the window of his car on the other side of the empty car park, where he sits in silence waiting for something. It is not long before Bright finally hears the muffled scuffling sounds that he has been waiting to hear, echoing through the night from the car in the corner of the car park.

He hears a scared squeal from Bagshott, which is then followed by a whimper. This is later followed by a cracking sound, which even frightens the headmaster for a moment until he hears another whimper from the over-eager parent before an eery silence descends over the whole of the car park.

Bright smiles an imperceptible smile as he winds up his window, because he knows the job has now been done. He starts his car, then drives slowly out of the car park.

In the quiet of the dark corner of the car park, Bagshott's car is now the only car there. There are no lights and no sounds that come from this corner of the car park and one would assume that the car had been parked here for the night.

However, slowly and imperceptibly at first, there are muffled sounds from the inside of Bagshott's thought-to-be-deserted car. Bagshott lies draped over the front seat of his car looking scuffed and bruised but there are pained moves from his limbs that suggest to him that he will be okay.

Bagshott can feel a pain all over his body as he lifts himself back into his front seat to check his face in the car mirror for damage. He nervously scans the empty car park for signs of the enemy through his mirror before quickly closing his car door and locking it. He then starts his car and drives swiftly out of the car park, knowing that he will never venture forth to another parent-teacher evening at this school ever again.

Chapter 14

Under a bright moon, two figures dressed in bee-keepers' outfits creep towards one of the larger and newer bee hives in the field near to the old bee hives. One of the figures then lifts the top off one of these grander bee hives, allowing a loud, deep hum from the encased bees to fill the night air.

"You're sure you know what you are doing?" asks Roger nervously.

"Shut up. Can you see the queen?" asks Heckton bluntly, while Roger shines his torch down into the opened hive to take a look.

"Not yet. Perhaps in the daylight I would have been able to," replies Roger.

"Here – I see it; as large a bee as I have ever seen," says Heckton, wide-eyed.

"You be careful with it," replies Roger.

"What do you think these thick rubber gloves are for?" says Heckton, putting his thick rubber gloved hands slowly inside the bee hive to pull out the queen bee.

The other rudely awoken bees quickly pepper Heckton's bee keeper's outfit to try to sting him but

Heckton remains strong and steady and pulls the queen bee fearlessly out of the bee hive to place it into a holdall that Roger reluctantly holds open just below him.

"She's a real beauty isn't she? She seems drowsy though, as if she's been on a long journey. Good job, too, because if she did try to sting me it would probably pierce this protective clothing quite easily," says Heckton knowledgeably, as he places the queen bee carefully inside the holdall then quickly zips the bag closed while swiping away the other attacking bees as best he can.

"Come on, let's get out of here," says Roger, while Heckton pulls open another holdall nearby. "We've got one of these buggers – let's not push our luck and try to get the other one, as well," Roger insists, now holding the zipped-up holdall containing the humming queen bee at a good arms-length.

However, Heckton has already removed the roof of the other large bee hive. He stands on a small ladder resting against it to reach down fearlessly once more into the hive to try and find the other large queen bee.

"If we're right," he says, reaching down with his thick rubber gloves on, "and we take away these queens, then the other bees may go back to the old hives and they will not produce so much of this suspect honey," says Heckton.

"This will protect our Year Elevens from Wade's do-gooding. Is that the plan?" replies Roger.

"That's the theory we'll go with, Little," says Heckton, as he pulls out a livelier and deeply humming queen bee from the other bee hive.

"We need to keep all of this between just the few of us for now, Roger. It is only a theory at the moment and we have no proof that what we're doing here is really upsetting Wade's master plan, but it is the lead that they want us to follow up," replies Heckton, while Roger flashes his powerful torch over Heckton's face just as he pulls the other queen bee clear of the bee hive.

"I say, where did you get that bruised face from, Heckton?" asks Roger, noticing the blackening around one of Heckton's eyes when the torchlight flashes over his face.

"Never you mind," replies Heckton angrily. "Just open the bag will you?"

"And who are we keeping this theory between? Who else is involved in tonight's little caper?" asks Roger, opening the bag to wait for Heckton to climb back down the ladder and place the bee inside it.

These constant questions from Roger, together with his torchlight flashing all over the place, soon unsteady Heckton from his perch and send him crashing down from his ladder onto the ground, releasing the queen bee that he held in his gloves back into the moonlit air.

"Ow! Ow! Ouch, ouch!" cries Heckton, when his head-protector flies off his head in the fall and a swarm of bees begin to sting his unprotected face.

Roger reacts quickly in the commotion. He somehow captures the queen be in his gloves in mid-flight, places it into the open holdall, then quickly zips it up. He then throws the head-protector that had fallen off Heckton's head quickly back towards Heckton, who writhes around on the ground in agony, so that he can hastily grab it and with very grateful hands try to put it back over his head while the bees continue to sting him.

Roger then grabs both holdalls containing the queen bees and makes a hasty retreat, because the now very agitated bees from both hives angrily pepper Roger's and Heckton's protective armour wherever they can.

In their escape, Roger's head-protector soon flies off his head, too. The angry bees race towards them with only one thing on their minds: to sting these two intruders into a retreat.

"Ouch, ouch, ouch!" cries Roger, swiping the bees away from his face as best he can, while fumbling around on the ground to try and find his head protection. He finally grabs hold of his head-protector in the darkness and puts it hastily back over his head. His face stings like mad and he can feel his cheeks swelling. Heckton soon emerges out of the darkness behind him and shines his torch into Roger's face.

"If you've got your head-protector on and we've got both of the queen bees, let's get out of here," says Heckton, now grabbing hold of one of the holdalls containing one of the large bees. Roger had no other intention on his mind. They dash away through the darkness under the moonlight with the large swarm of bees in pursuit.

"These are persistent little buggers! Why don't these chasing bees give up?" cries Heckton, when he feels a sting to one of his arms.

They run on through the field until they can see Heckton's jeep parked just ahead of them, behind some trees. Heckton arrives first and hastily opens the doors to his jeep with the swarm of bees still in close pursuit.

"I thought you said these bees will go back to the other hives once the queens have been removed? Why are they still chasing us?" asks Roger.

"I don't know. Ask them!" replies Heckton, diving into his car seat then slamming his car door closed. Roger soon arrives at the passenger door. He jumps inside the car with the bees swarming around his head. He throws his holdall onto the back seat then closes his jeep door, with the bees still buzzing around their heads inside the locked car.

"There's still too many of them inside the jeep with us. Keep your head gear on!" shouts Roger, as some of the bees find ways through Roger's and Heckton's protective clothes to sting them all over their bodies.

Heckton wheelspins his jeep out of the field, skids back onto the country lane, then speeds away as fast as he can with a swarm of chasing bees still outside their vehicle in constant pursuit.

Heckton eventually drives his jeep slowly up the driveway to his house, then turns off the ignition. There's still a very deep, low hum coming from both holdalls on the back seat, as well as a more annoying hum coming from the bees that surround both of their heads inside the car.

Both of them search outside for the chasing swarm of bees but neither of them can see any sign of them.

"I'll open the front door, then you follow me in. There's a porch door inside the front door, so we can hopefully keep these other bees from entering the main house. Then we're home free," says Heckton, looking Roger in the eyes.

"I've never seen queen bees this large before, anywhere. Are you sure you know how to handle them?" asks Roger, looking very worried.

"There's a shed in my back garden. I'll keep them in there until we know what we should do with them," replies Heckton, getting out of his jeep.

"You know, taking these bees will stir things up nicely at school," adds Heckton, baring his teeth with delight.

"What do you mean, 'stir things up'? I'm doing all this to prevent Rose getting herself into any more trouble. If there's going to be a sacking at the end of term, it should only be Wade's. That's why I am helping you," replies Roger looking at him. "And for the sake of the school of course," he adds.

"Yes, of course, Roger," says Heckton, with a menacing grin on his face. "We can take these queen bees around to the headmaster's home tomorrow evening, so that he can make plenty of honey for himself to put on his toast at breakfast time," adds Heckton, chuckling nastily.

Roger looks more worried than ever. He always had doubts about helping Heckton and now his suspicions about him increase. He even wonders whether stealing these queen bees has been Heckton's idea and has nothing to do with the headmaster at all.

"Oh, my face feels very sore. Does it look sore?" asks Roger.

"Come on, we'll put these queen bees inside my shed then you can get lost. I mean, go home," says Heckton.

Heckton and Roger have just stepped out of Heckton's jeep when they notice the swarm of chasing bees that they had almost forgotten about fly around the corner of the road just ahead of them.

They both jump back inside the car and slam their doors closed just before the approaching swarm of bees pepper their front windscreen. They look to each other, wondering what do next. The front door of Heckton's house is tantalisingly close yet the bees swarm around the doors of their jeep preventing them from getting there. Curtains soon begin to twitch in the bedrooms of neighbouring houses all the way along Heckton's street.

Geoff takes a seat next to Rose in the staffroom the next morning, just before Roger walks through the door into the staff room behind him. Poor Roger's face is covered with red stings from the bees that make one side of his head appear very swollen. Geoff freezes when he sees Roger. He stares at Roger's face knowing big trouble is afoot. Rose feels the same way.

"So that's what Roger was up to last night. I wondered where he had got to," says Rose to a deeply worried-looking Geoff.

Geoff remains silent while his mind works overtime. He's about to go over to Roger to find out what happened to him last night and to try and arrange a hasty cover-up story that would not attract any more attention from anyone at the school, when Max Heckton strides into the staff room with a similarly red swollen face from all of the bee stings from the night before.

Geoff feels completely dumbstruck by the sight of Roger and Heckton. He knows that deep trouble is on the way. He looks to the door and wonders if a quick exit would be the best solution, given the circumstances.

"Oh no, Geoff. . . What have those two been up to, I wonder?" asks Rose.

"That's what I'm wondering too," replies Geoff. "And if it doesn't involve Russell Appleby, then we've been very lucky indeed," adds Geoff, knowing all too well that their plans for the summer exams could well be in jeopardy. He immediately wonders whether Russell Appleby could be in a similarly stung way.

"Well, let me take a guess, Geoff," sighs Rose.

"They're both going to upset our plans big time," replies Geoff under his breath.

"Yep, very likely and in a very big way," says Rose.

"But that's not good for either of us; not good at all," replies Geoff.

"No, not good for either of us," repeats Rose, sighing a very deep sigh. "And I can't believe Roger's got involved with that Heckton in any way whatsoever. I've told him about that before," adds Rose.

For the moment, both Heckton and Roger take seats and say nothing to any of the other teachers despite being looked at intensely. They both wait for the headmaster to enter the room to give the morning's briefing, while the other teachers stare at the pair of them with interest but wisely do not say anything for fear of putting their feet into something that they may later regret.

Even though Geoff feels as panicked as Rose, each of them sitting on the opposite side of the room from the red-faced pair, he can't help himself from chuckling at the sight of the two red, swollen faces that look at him angrily from across the staff room.

It's not long before Anthony Bright strides into the staff room with his black gown billowing out behind him. He immediately spots the two likely lads with their swollen faces sitting to one side. He is forced to stop mid-stride and address the pair of them.

"Max, Roger – I need to see you both immediately after today's briefing," says Bright, giving Heckton a very questioningly look indeed. "On second thoughts, you can't teach looking like that. I will see you both first thing tomorrow morning. Go home," he orders, looking very angry.

Later that morning, Geoff sits at his desk, marking books, while his Year Eleven pupils sit hard at work in front of him. He thinks he must contact Appleby at break time to find out what happened at his farmhouse last night, if anything.

Halfway through his lesson, something makes him look up from his books. He finds Tomkins staring out of the window just ahead of him. Geoff is about to tell him to get back to his work, when he notices Tomkins' mouth suddenly drop open with wonder – or is it fright?

Outside the window, in the school grounds, Russell Appleby jumps down from out of the sky to land in the middle of the playground. Appleby then crouches on the ground, using one hand to steady himself, superhero-style, and looks around his environs with an angry scowl all over his face.

Inside the school classroom, Tomkins jumps to his feet when he witnesses Appleby jump out of the sky, wearing his tweed jacket, then land so expertly in the middle of the playground.

"What the–! Who's that? It's that farmer, Mr Appleby! Did you see that? How did he do that?" cries

Tomkins with astonishment, making Geoff look out of his window, as well as causing the other pupils to do likewise.

"He just jumped out of the sky into the middle of the playground. He can fly! Mr Appleby can fly!" adds Tomkins, making the situation all the more exciting and all the more difficult for Geoff to control, because the other pupils jump out of their seats wanting to take a look out of the window.

"Okay, class – just get back to your work. This has nothing to do with you," replies Geoff, trying to keep order, but failing.

In the classroom next door, Arthur Crook addresses his students with trigonometry diagrams drawn all over the blackboard behind him. When Crook instantly notices Appleby land on the school playground outside, through the window, his eyes immediately light up with excitement.

"Ah hah," says Crook, as if he has been waiting for something like this to happen ever since he started working at the school, or perhaps, his whole life. "What do we have here?" he adds, rushing towards the window to find Appleby crouching on the playground outside. "Class, get on with your work. I will be back very soon," he adds, dashing towards the door of his classroom, eyes wide with the prospect of finding out just who has landed so extraordinarily on the playground outside his classroom.

Crook slams open the outside door of the school then strides purposefully towards Appleby, who is still scanning the whole school from his crouching position on the playground.

Crook remains fearless when he approaches Appleby, despite the farmer looking as angry as he has ever seen anyone. He's too excited to feel fear at the moment because he knows that uncovering the truth of the rumours he was sent in to investigate at this school could be just the making of him.

"Just stop right there – is it Russell Appleby? If it is, I know all about you. I've been briefed about you. So you are involved in the little caper going on at this school?" says Crook.

"Who are you?" replies Appleby, not fearing this funny little man who is approaching him so energetically.

"My name is Arthur Crook, school inspector, and you are now under arrest," says Crook, not really thinking about what he is saying.

"Under arrest? What for?" questions Appleby, half expecting Crook to produce a pair of handcuffs at any minute.

"For jumping out of the sky and landing in the school playground?" replies Crook. "How exactly did you manage that? Jumping out of the sky like that? And what exactly are you doing here? You are a local farmer, if I remember my brief correctly," adds Crook, feeling the adrenalin rush through his body.

Appleby quickly becomes annoyed by this annoying little man. "Where is Geoff Wade? I need to talk to him," asks Appleby.

"Ah hah, Wade is it? So he is involved, too? Just as I thought," replies Crook, as the little plot he had been sent in to investigate slowly reveals itself to him.

Just before Appleby pushes Crook out of his way, Geoff strides out of the school door and approaches both of them.

"Geoff, where are my queen bees?" says Appleby, too fuming to say anything else just at the moment. "If something has happened to my queen bees. . ."

"Bees? Queen bees, is it? And just where might these queen bees be right now?" pipes up Crook, unable to stay quiet.

Appleby stares angrily at Geoff, while Geoff tries to plead silently with Appleby to remain quiet on the subject in front of Crook. However, Appleby doesn't pick up on the signals and is too angry to keep quiet on the subject of his precious queen bees, anyway.

Crook is incensed and determined to put these two behind bars as soon as he can. He grabs Geoff's shirt collar and tries to manhandle him away, despite being much smaller than him.

"Just what do you think you're doing, Crook? This doesn't concern you. Go back inside the school. You're new to the school and have no idea what is going on here. Leave me to deal with this. I know Appleby and what this is all about," replies Geoff, freeing himself easily from Crook's hold.

"It was you last night, wasn't it, at my farmhouse? You're the culprit. You stole my prize queen bees?" says Appleby angrily.

"Steal your queen bees? Of course it wasn't me who stole your bees. Why would I do that?" replies Geoff.

"Stealing his prize bees last night, were you, Geoff? It doesn't surprise me in the least. And just what would you be wanting to steal his prize queen bees for?" asks Crook, knowing he has hit upon gold dust and sure it will mean a big promotion for him amongst his school-inspecting fraternity, when he puts these two likely lads behind bars.

"Let me assure, you, Mr Wade, that if you have stolen his queen bees it will be the last time you will steal any more bees while working as a teacher," adds Crook threateningly.

Appleby approaches Geoff angrily and they can both sense a fight is about to happen.

"I know who stole your bees," says Geoff. "I know who was at your farmhouse last night. In fact, I was going to contact you today about it," he adds, hoping to calm down the red-faced and angry-looking Appleby as he grabs hold of his shirt collar.

Appleby's too angry to listen to anything Geoff has to say and he's just about to throw his first angry punch towards him when Geoff feels forced to reveal the culprits, even in front of this brave little school inspector standing close between them to try and avert a confrontation.

"It was Heckton and Little. They stole your two precious bees," replies Geoff.

"Who are they?" asks Appleby.

"They're both teachers at this school. You've met Roger. They're the culprits. But I suggest you don't try and talk to them right now," says Geoff, still eyeing Crook.

"Goodness gracious, the whole school's in on your little scheme, Geoff? There will be hell to pay for this if that is the case," adds Crook.

"Get lost, Crook," says Geoff, now so annoyed by his presence that he pushes Crook to the ground.

Crook immediately gets back to his feet. "I've been sent here to investigate the unusual grades that many of the students at this school have been getting in their mock exams and I'm pleased to tell you that I will have the pleasure in unmasking you all when I get to the bottom of this. I will close this school down if it's the last thing I do," says Crook bravely, knowing that he could well have uncovered a hornets' nest of trouble.

It is now Appleby's turn to push Crook to the ground, just as Max Heckton's pus-filled, bee-stung face emerges out of the school and paces towards the three of them to try and stir things up even more. Headmaster, Anthony Bright, soon appears in the doorway just behind Heckton, holding his head in anguish.

Heckton is never been one to avoid a confrontation if a confrontation can be made out of nothing, so when he sees the fracas in the playground he strides towards Appleby and the others, looking hopeful for trouble.

"What are you doing inside the school grounds? You want some, Appleby. You want some trouble? You got some trouble. . ." says Heckton, balling up one of his hands into a fist.

Appleby's never been approached so angrily like this before and despite feeling as angry as Heckton, he can immediately tell that he doesn't have the experience in confrontations that this approaching menace, Heckton, obviously has.

Appleby does not know what to do. He can't run and jump away because they would hold him back and he knows that he is the one that has started it all by landing in the playground. He's stuck between a rock and a hard place. So he's forced to wait for Heckton to arrive and push his head against his own head with aggression. Appleby soon feels the full force of Heckton's bursting, pus-filled sores, which drip onto the head of the farmer as he falls to the ground.

Appleby is not defeated. He wipes his face clean of the pus then gets back to his feet and returns a surprisingly powerful head butt to Heckton, just as the headmaster strides towards the excited group standing in the middle of the playground.

Being taller than the others, Bright feels it is his duty to break up the angry pair involved in the confrontation. He forces the always rabid-looking Heckton away to get some distance between Heckton and Appleby.

"Max, get back inside the school. I thought I told you to go home," says the headmaster.

"You've got trouble and I'm a hell-load of trouble and you've got it, Appleby. Do you understand me?" shouts Heckton, while Bright tries to keep him away at arms' length.

Geoff has been keeping a slight distance after seeing Heckton flare up so quickly but he is as flustered as the others by now, so he pushes Appleby away to try to calm things between the pair of them so that the headmaster can try and regain control of the situation.

"You too, Geoff. Get back inside the school and leave this for me to deal with," says Bright commandingly.

No one moves or backs down for a short while and there's a tense stand-off between all of them. Even the headmaster is not sure what to do next. Bright and Geoff stand between Max Heckton and Appleby to keep them both apart, while Crook looks on excitedly from the sidelines but stays right amongst them all despite being shorter than the rest of them.

The tense stand-off lasts for some time and the headmaster is the first to realise that there is a calmness that is gradually seeping into all of them. So the longer it goes on like this, the calmer everyone will eventually get, he hopes.

Bright soon senses when that moment of adequate calm has arrived. He approaches the culprit of the current fracas, Appleby, while gesturing to Heckton and Geoff to walk guiltily back towards the school, now that they have calmed down enough to see sense, but leaves Arthur Crook to stay close to his long billowing gown so that he can lap up the unfolding drama with glee.

Inside the school corridors, pupils clamber over each at the windows to try and get a better look at what's going on outside in the playground. Rose and Roger stand back from the clambering students to try and keep some kind of order while the drama in the playground unfolds.

"You and Heckton were both at Appleby's place last night?" asks Rose.

"We've been spying on you and Geoff for a while now. We knew you and Geoff were up to something at his farmhouse," replies Roger. "We took two of the large bees from his bee hives when we discovered that they were going to be delivered," adds Roger.

"You did what? Why on earth did you do that, Roger?" asks Rose perplexed. "I can't believe you would do such a thing!"

"Max told me that he had been told by the headmaster that we should take some of the queen bees away. It would slow down the production of the honey and mean less honey being supplied to the pupils. That's the theory we were working with last night. We had figured out that it is Appleby's honey that you are putting into these drinks that you give the pupils," informs Roger.

"You say the headmaster told you to do this? I very much doubt that, Roger. The headmaster would never get involved in such a scheme. This is all Max Heckton's doing, I'm sure of it, and I told you before to keep well away from him at all times," replies Rose firmly.

"Whoever's idea it was, Rose, I'm convinced that it was right. I have to put a stop to Geoff's little scheme, to protect you, Rose. It's all done for you, you do know that, don't you?" replies Roger, while a pus-filled sore bursts open on his face.

"Oh, Roger," replies Rose, looking into his eyes.

"I'm sorry about Geoff and all that but we had no choice. I agree with Heckton. We had to take action to prevent you from ruining the reputation of this school, so we had to steal those two queen bees," replies Roger. "Can't you see that?"

"Roger! You can't possibly agree with Heckton, on anything, ever. You know, from the sounds of it, it was Heckton's idea all along to steal those queen bees, wasn't it?" asks Rose.

"Of course it wasn't Heckton's idea. These orders came right from the very top; from the headmaster himself," replies Roger, looking at Rose while he questions the orders in his mind.

"It's very obvious to me now that it was all Heckton's idea," Rose persists. "Why on earth would the headmaster suggest such a thing? If he was found out to have given these instructions to you, he would be instantly sacked. All it would take is for one of you to speak out against him. This has certainly all been Heckton's doing and he has done it to upset things at the school as much as possible. That's Heckton's real agenda, did you know that, Roger?"

"That can't possibly be Heckton's agenda. Why would he suggest such a thing? He is close to the headmaster. He's a teacher, Rose. That is why I listen to him," replies Roger.

Rose sighs a deep sigh when another pus-filled sore erupts on Roger's face. "I think you'll find that Heckton's a real piece of work. In fact, most of us teachers know that already, apart from you, it seems," she says.

"I don't agree. How many years has Heckton been teaching at this school? Anyway, whatever he is like we must always put the pupils' education first. We must think of their wellbeing above our own," adds Roger commendably.

"Exactly, Roger – think about the pupils, will you? They're all getting great grades at the moment," says Rose. "You wouldn't want to spoil that now, would you?"

Rose can't bear to argue with Roger any more. She can see that the pupils have got bored with the goings-on outside and have stopped clambering at the corridor windows, so she walks away from Roger in a huff leaving him to stand there, on his own, looking out of the window towards the playground with pus oozing down the side of his face.

He can see through the window that while Bright confronts Appleby, the short Arthur Crook keeps them both deep in conversation in the middle of the playground. As he wonders whether he should join them outside and support the headmaster, another pus-filled sore bursts open on his face.

Outside in the playground, Bright, Appleby and Crook seem to have cooled down a little since Geoff and Heckton sloped back indoors.

"Headmaster, I've got a business to run and someone is trying to sabotage it," says Appleby finally.

"What business is that? What are you talking about, Russell? It certainly doesn't give you the right to jump into the school grounds during school time looking, to all intents and purposes, like someone we pay the police to protect us against, tweed jacket or no tweed jacket," replies Bright.

"Headmaster, you are right. This man is trespassing on school land and during the school day," adds Crook.

"Oh, do be quiet, Arthur," replies Bright curtly.

Bright eventually notices the commotion amongst the pupils inside the school out of the corner of his eye. He must act to remedy this problem straight away. "Actually, Crook's right, you are trespassing and if you don't get out of my school this instant, I shall call the police. Your business problems can wait until after the school day," replies the headmaster firmly.

"At last, a firm hand and some sense. I will call the police for you, headmaster," says Crook.

Appleby can now see he is on the losing side in all of this and soon realises that he has made an error in his judgment, allowing his anger to get the better of him. He knows that it will be best to confront Geoff out of school hours. So, without another word, he runs away from Bright and Crook then jumps high and far, right out of the school grounds, with one enormous lunge.

Headmaster Bright and Arthur Crook look up into the sky when Appleby disappears from sight, with their jaws wide open with shock. They look to each other as if to say, 'Did you see that?', but when neither of them say anything about it, they get back to their senses as quickly as they can, then walk back towards the school while they both try to come to terms with what they have just witnessed.

"You see! Madness, complete and utter madness. I sensed it as soon as I walked into your school on the first day of term," says Crook finally.

"Just go back to your class, Arthur, and pretend that this didn't happen," says Bright sensibly.

"I can't do that, headmaster. You must be aware by now that I am an undercover school inspector sent in to investigate the rumours about Year Eleven's inflated grades in their mock exams. And what I have just seen cannot go unreported. In fact, I may have to close your school down because of it," says Crook, feeling the power he may soon possess flow through his body.

"Perhaps it would be best, when you have calmed your pupils down and set them work for the rest of the lesson, to return to my office where we can discuss this matter further," says Bright, getting very annoyed by the presence of this little man prying into his domain.

Bright then opens the door to allow Crook back inside, while he huffs to himself before following him back into the school.

Chapter 15

Several days after the commotion in the playground and late into the evening, Geoff drives his battered, old car through the darkness with Rose sitting next to him.

In the back seat sits Roger Little and they all wear bee-keeper's protection outfits with their head-protectors placed next to Roger on the back seat.

Geoff turns his car into Max Heckton's street and they cruise along until Roger thinks he recognises Heckton's house.

"I've got to thank you for helping us like this, Roger," says Geoff.

"It is the only right thing Roger should be doing," replies Rose. "Once I had convinced him that Heckton works to his own agenda most of the time, I knew we would have to get those bees back before the headmaster finds out and gets involved. If we don't, I'm sure it will mean the whole school will suffer because of it."

"You're forgetting about Crook. He'll be sniffing around us, eager to spill the beans to the headmaster if he discovers anything more about our plans," adds Roger.

"That is why we have to react quickly and get those bees back to Appleby as soon as we can. If we do that, Appleby will be happy and we can continue with our scheme to bathe our Year Elevens in glory," says Geoff.

"I don't think Heckton would try to get the headmaster into trouble if he could help it," says Roger. "They were in the desert together, apparently – whatever that means," adds Roger.

"Heckton has his own agenda now. He doesn't get on with the headmaster anymore and I don't think he will be prepared to protect the headmaster again if it interferes with any of his ideas. The headmaster is bound to become involved if we don't get those bees back to Appleby's farmhouse as soon as we can," replies Rose.

Roger winds his car window down and breathes in some late spring air until he can hear the deep humming of the bees coming from Heckton's house.

"This is Heckton's place," says Roger. "I can hear them humming," he adds.

"Yes, I can hear them, too. Ex marks the spot then," says Geoff, parking his car on the opposite side of the street.

"You are sure Heckton's out?" adds Geoff.

"Susan finally got him to go out with her," says Rose.

"You know, this is all getting a bit serious, Geoff, breaking into someone's house like this. We should return these bees and then leave Appleby well alone," says Roger, very seriously. "You can't go ahead with your plans for the summer exams. I'm risking enough coming with you here tonight. I will be forced to tell the headmaster of your plans if you don't stop after this."

Geoff is about to argue with him, when Rose puts her hand on his arm to pacify him and prevent him from saying anything more, at least for tonight.

Once their car is parked, Roger hands the other two their bee-keepers' head gear, then they all pile out of their car as quietly as they can and head for Heckton's place on the opposite side of the street.

It is dark and well past midnight, so they hope that none of the neighbours' curtains will begin to twitch when they get down to business. Geoff tries the high side-gate first but finds it locked. He can hear the hum of the bees very closely on the other side of the gate, so he expertly climbs over it, then unlocks it from the other side allowing Roger and Rose to slink through and close it behind them.

Geoff puts on his rubber gloves, then approaches the small shed where the humming emanates from.

"They're in here, Roger. What were you and Heckton going to do with the bees after you had put them in here?" asks Geoff.

"I've no idea," replies Roger.

"You see, Roger – then it must have been Heckton's idea all along," Rose adds.

"Anything to stir up trouble – that's Heckton," adds Rose.

"Right, are you ready?" says Geoff, just before breaking the lock on the shed door and opening it, allowing a swarm of angry bees to quickly pepper their bee-keeper's outfits to try to sting them.

"These bumble bees must have followed these queens all the way here from Appleby's farm. Clever, huh? The queens will be well protected so prepare for a quick exit," adds Geoff knowledgeably, previously having seen Appleby working at his hives.

Once Geoff has scanned the state of play inside the shed, he and Rose step inside with their eyes open wide with fear, but so far not yet stung. They search the shed with their torchlight until they finally spot the large queen bees, covered with bumble bees, in opposite corners of the shed.

"Aghh! Look at the size of those things! They look even bigger than when I last saw them," says Geoff, moving slowly towards one of the queens in one corner while the surrounding bumble bees intensify their stinging quest.

Geoff fearlessly reaches for the queen bee with his thick rubber gloves, causing a rake to fall to the floor just in front of him in the darkness that, in turn, makes him stumble and leave a bare patch of skin on his back which the bees readily go to sting.

"Ouch, ouch, ow!" cries Geoff, before re-covering his bare patch of back.

The queen bee consequently easily escapes from Geoff's rubber-gloved fumbling and flies straight towards Rose. Rose screams when it heads her way. She falls to the floor and drops her torch in the process, leaving the queen bee to hum easily out of the shed door and away into the night.

"Damn it!" says Geoff, watching the queen bee disappear from sight. "Roger, bring the holdall into the shed, will you?" he says hurriedly.

Roger throws the opened holdall into the shed; he's not going to risk entering the shed himself.

Geoff is determined not to let the other queen bee escape at the opposite end of the shed, so he closes in on it quickly, despite the relentless peppering of bees on his protector outfit.

His determination soon pays off. He grabs the other queen bee first time inside his rubber gloves. He then quickly throws the bee into the holdall and zips the bag up, despite more bees stinging his body where they have found weaknesses in his protective clothing.

"Let's go!" says Geoff, quickly carrying the holdall with the merchandise inside out of the shed.

Geoff, Rose and Roger then race back towards the high wooden gate in Heckton's back garden. They open it then dash through the darkness back towards Geoff's car on the other side of the street. Rose follows him as closely as she can and leaves Roger to re-lock the gate behind them.

Despite the lateness of the hour, several neighbours' curtains do begin to twitch when they hear the agitated humming coming from Heckton's back garden but fortunately for Geoff and his gang, they're all too sleepy to make out the intruders or the car when everything goes quiet again.

Geoff opens his car door then throws the holdall with the queen bee inside it onto the back seat. He tries to start the engine as quickly as he can, while Rose swiftly climbs into the back seat to guard the holdall. Roger soon races across the street as fast as he can before the swarm of angry escaped bees chase after him in pursuit of their stolen queen.

Roger jumps into the passenger seat and closes his car door just before the swarm of bees pepper their windscreen. At first, Geoff has trouble starting his old car but once he has, he wheel-spins the car away along the street as rapidly as he can while several bees hum around inside their car, trying to sting them wherever they can. As their car drives away, the swarm of escaped bees fly through the air just behind them in pursuit.

Geoff's car soon skids out of Heckton's street at the top of the hill, then disappears around the corner into the darkness, just as Max Heckton drives his jeep around the corner at the other end of the street with Susan Chalmers sitting lovingly next to him.

Heckton soon spots a large, dark mass move through the air under the street lights just ahead and his eyes immediately widen with anger. He can't help but think of the bees in his shed, so he skids his car hurriedly to a halt in his driveway, then bounds out of it towards his front door. Heckton fumes with anger when he looks towards the disappearing dark mass of bees at the top of his street.

Inside Geoff's car, Rose holds the holdall with her rubber gloves on to keep it as still as she can, while Geoff drives his car speedily through the suburban streets, continually swiping away bees that hover around their heads.

"Heckton's not going to be happy about this tomorrow morning," says Roger.

"You stay well clear of Heckton tomorrow, Roger. In fact, it would be best if you took the day off because of your sting sores and all," replies Rose.

"You know, Rose is right, Roger,' agrees Geoff. "The headmaster would never have asked Heckton to steal those queen bees. What does Bright know about all of this, anyway? Heckton's been snooping and spying on us and that's how he knows what he knows but the headmaster, I'm guessing, hasn't a clue about any of it. And Rose is right: Heckton likes causing trouble. I'm sure that's the real reason why he wanted to steal the queen bees from Appleby's place."

"What about Roger's and Heckton's bee stung faces?" asks Rose. "The headmaster has seen those."

"The headmaster never got round to talking to us about our sore faces because he was too busy," says Roger.

"You can be so naive, Roger," replies Rose. "The headmaster will surely ask you about your faces when Heckton raises a stink tomorrow morning. You must stay away from school for at least a few days. The headmaster will soon forget all about your spotty faces," adds Rose.

"I'll take this queen bee back to Appleby's farm right now. And, you know, we must find that other queen bee before anyone else does," says Geoff.

"Oh, Geoff, what have we done? We've got ourselves into this mess right up to our necks, which I knew we would do," sighs Rose.

"Rose is right about you taking time off," says Geoff. "You make sure you take the day off tomorrow, Roger, for sure. It would be for the best; the best for all of us. Your face still looks very sore."

"I can't take the day off," replies Roger.

"Why can't you?" asks Geoff.

"What about the students? How will they cope without me there to guide them, especially at this time of year?" replies Roger.

"For once in your life, Roger, forget about your students. Think about yourself and what is best for you, just this once, will you?" replies Rose, almost ready to sigh again.

"What you really mean is to think about you and what's best for you two," replies Roger.

Rose looks to Roger in the front seat as pus oozes from his face sores and begins to seep through his head-protection gear, while more bees find their way under his head gear to sting his face some more. She begins to sob a little as Geoff's old car splutters through a suburban street with the swarm of bees still in close pursuit behind them.

Chapter 16

Very early in the morning, a week or two later, just as the first light shines over Honibridge Modern, a figure creeps along an empty school corridor until he reaches Geoff Wade's classroom.

He unlocks the classroom door, then creeps through the room towards the desk where he begins to hurriedly search through the drawers until he pulls out a set of keys. With these keys glinting in the early morning sun shining in through the window, he makes his way towards the cupboard at the back of the classroom.

The unseen figure opens the cupboard, pulls away a pile of books, then reaches in and pulls out a large and dusty bottle of blackcurrant juice that sits hidden behind them all. Once he has taken the bottle of blackcurrant juice out of the cupboard, the hidden figure re-locks the cupboard door then creeps quietly out of the classroom and re-locks the classroom door behind him.

The mysterious man then disappears into the mists of the corridor ahead with the precious bottle of blackcurrant juice under his arm.

Later that day, Max Heckton stands behind his desk in his classroom with a furtive look all over his slightly less-reddened, stung and sore face. He pulls out the mysterious bottle of blackcurrant juice that he had procured earlier that morning and then looks to the pupils seated ahead of him. He ponders only for a short moment before pouring the blackcurrant juice, together with some water from a jug that he had prepared earlier, into some beakers laid out on his desk just as the bell rings for break time.

"Now, class, some refreshments for you now that it is the summer term," says Heckton, hiding his evil, toothy grin behind his lips.

His Year Eleven pupils seated in front of him, Thompson, Andrews and Jordan amongst them, have become used to this refreshment routine now but they still feel slightly apprehensive about going to the front to collect their beakers, because this is the first time that Heckton has offered them refreshments.

It doesn't take too long for one pupil to make his way to the front, whereupon they all soon pile around Heckton's desk, eager to partake of the blackcurrant juice before rushing outside into the playground for break time.

After all of the pupils have gone outside to play, Heckton returns to his desk to hastily throw away the empty blackcurrant juice bottle and to empty the jug of remaining water into a sink nearby. Heckton then takes a seat at his desk with a teeth-filled grin all over his face.

Outside in the playground the pupils dash around as usual to begin with but it's not long before several of them begin to feel the effects of the specially honeyed blackcurrant juice that Geoff had doctored weeks ago and almost forgotten about.

Thompson's the first to feel lighter than usual and when he jumps, he can feel his body rise into the air for much longer than would be normal if he hadn't drunk the honeyed juice in the first place.

With astonishment, Andrews watches Thompson's huge leaps that take him almost across the width of the playground. He feels he may be able to do the same, so he tries it and sure enough, he finds he can jump just as far and as high as Thompson just did, moments earlier.

They both look at each other with feelings of astonishment at the newly acquired miraculous abilities that they both find they are now capable of, so they both try these running lunges once again and this time they find that they can jump higher and further than before.

It is not long before all the pupils that have just had their refreshments provided for them by Heckton run and jump high and far around the playground just like Andrews and Thompson continue to do with relish.

"Whoaaah!" cries Thompson, when his jump takes him into the branches of a nearby tree.

"Here, let me try!" says Andrews, as his leap takes him onto the top of a nearby, low-roofed school outbuilding. It is not long before Heckton's Year Eleven pupils all jump as high as the roof of the school buildings around them, taking some of them higher into the branches of nearby trees, leaving the teachers on playground duty below to open their mouths with shock, then rush inside to inform the headmaster.

Heckton, by now, is far too clued-up on Geoff's little scheme and all too well aware of the effects that the doctored blackcurrant juice may have on his pupils, that he doesn't blink twice when he looks towards the leaping students just outside his window. However, he does grab the empty blackcurrant juice container from the rubbish bin, then take it out of his classroom and throw it into the back of a spare cupboard further along the corridor, because he is still a little surprised by the strong effects it is having on his pupils in the playground.

It doesn't take long for the teachers whose rooms overlook the playground and who witness the astonishing scenes outside, take action by dashing out of their classrooms and striding towards the headmaster's office on the top floor of the building.

Arthur Crook is one of those teachers whose room overlooks the playground and he stares for a minute, in total shock, open-mouthed, at the jumping and leaping students outside .

"This is just ridiculous!" he finally declares to no one in particular, while his pupils in front of him begin to laugh out loud when they see their friends perched high up in the trees just outside their classroom.

"Right! You all need to stay seated, class, for your own protection. I will be back in a minute," cries Crook, storming out of his classroom, more determined than ever to close this school down as soon as he can when the root of the problem has been discovered.

Geoff looks towards the playground from his classroom window, equally horrified, and immediately wonders if Rose may have given her pupils some of the blackcurrant juice, forgetting that it shouldn't be given to them just before break times when the exercise will cause their limbs to be affected instead of their minds.

In the classroom next door to Geoff's, Roger looks out over the playground, in equal amounts of horror, just as the final, unhealed, pus-filled sore on his face bursts open with the stress. Roger dashes out of his classroom and meets Geoff in the corridor, where they both look equally as flustered and wonder what they should do next.

In the headmaster's office on the top floor of the school building, Anthony Bright is sitting soberly at his desk, working through several papers in front of him, until something catches his attention out of the corner of his eye. He looks up from his work to witness Sarah Jordan appear outside his office window, three floors up from the ground. She smiles at him then disappears from sight, equally as quickly.

Bright rubs his eyes, puts his glasses back on, then gets back to his work, only for his attention to be grabbed for a second time when he sees Sarah Jordan's face once more appear outside his window, then disappear again. Bright storms to his feet and knows something is very wrong.

He dashes towards his office window only to see Jordan's astonished, bright face stare right into his for a brief moment then disappear again. Bright immediately opens the window of his office and looks down over the playground below him.

"Great Scott!" exclaims Bright, when he sees two dozen jumping and leaping students in the playground below. "What the dickens is going on?" he adds, before storming towards the closed door of his office.

In the playground, several teachers try to restrain the Year Eleven pupils still remaining on the ground but they have little success and Thompson and Andrews have jumped so high up into the trees that they have absolutely no way of getting down.

They leave more of their classmates standing on top of the low-roofed outbuildings around them, as well as a few of their class mates, standing right on top of the roof of the school, terrified out of their wits when they look downwards towards the teachers below.

Geoff and Roger run into the playground and immediately try to restrain one of Heckton's Year Elevens who runs towards them but the boy has too much energy and wriggles himself free, then runs and leaps into a tree to escape.

The headmaster finally arrives on the scene with half a dozen irate teachers hovering around him. He looks around the playground with absolute dismay and wonders how he will ever survive this little prank.

However, headmaster Bright is not the headmaster for nothing and he soon takes command, herding some of the more compliant Year Elevens back inside the school as quickly as he can, before joining Geoff and Roger nearer to the trees, both determined to help the headmaster with his task.

"What the Scott's going on, Geoff?" demands Bright, looking at Geoff and knowing he must have the answer, which he does but he doesn't let on, even though the headmaster himself can tell Geoff knows. Geoff and Roger just shrug their shoulders at the headmaster as if to say they have no idea what is afoot.

It is at this moment that Geoff spies Heckton stride out of the school with his evil, toothy grin clearly on display and it is now that the horror of what must have happened hits Geoff, almost like a painful slap around the face.

Someone must have found that full bottle of old, doctored blackcurrant juice that Geoff had completely forgotten about, having hidden it in his cupboard weeks and weeks ago. He immediately knows it must have been Heckton who found it, so he dashes towards him feeling quite terrified.

"What have you done, Heckton?" asks Geoff.

"What has me, done? Me has done nothing," replies Heckton, chuckling, just as one of his unhealed pus-filled sores on his face explodes, bringing his chuckling to an abrupt end.

Geoff's fear soon turns to anger, for their plans for the summer exams surely now lie in ruins after this. He lays into Heckton, bringing him to the ground and forcing them to tussle on the grass.

Roger bounds over to try to separate them but they fight so intensely that he cannot bring a stop to it.

"Stop this at once, you two!" says Roger, to no effect, as fire-engine sirens begin to sound in the far distance.

"If you two do not break up this fighting, I will be forced to tell the headmaster," says Roger ineffectually.

Geoff and Heckton continue to fight and Roger starts to get very worried. He looks to the headmaster on the opposite side of the playground but he can see he is fully occupied with herding the affected pupils, who still stand on terra firma, back into the school. Roger tries to physically break up their tussle himself, one more time, but with no success.

It is not long after that, that two noisy fire engines pull into the school car park and firemen soon buzz around the playground trying to locate the errant school children trapped in the trees and on top of roofs all around them. Geoff and Heckton finally stop fighting, when they see and hear the fire engines pull into their school.

One of the fire engines is forced to drive into the playground itself. Its ladder soon rises and extends towards the tree where Thompson and Andrews sit nervously. They have managed to jump the highest out of all of their class mates and because of it, they look the most scared, too.

With a fireman quickly climbing the extended ladder, it is not long before the brave fireman ushers Thompson and Andrews down the ladder back onto the safety of the playground.

The other fire engine is forced to drive into the school playground, too, so that the firemen can bring down the many other pupils still perched high up on the rooftops of the school's outbuildings.

When the last of the Year Elevens has finally been brought safely back down to earth, headmaster Bright breathes out a huge sigh of relief. Roger, Geoff and Heckton then guiltily help the headmaster herd the most wayward and most adventurous pupils, faces white with fear, back inside the school. The headmaster, Geoff, Roger and Heckton then say nothing to each other for a good long while after being stunned into shock.

Finally, it is left to Heckton to get angry once more with a rage he cannot restrain, which is not unusual for him. He squares up to Geoff right in front of the headmaster.

"This is the last time you step on my shoes, Wade. You're finished," says Heckton. Geoff angers, too, but the headmaster, aided by Roger, keeps them both well apart.

"Have you two quite finished? says Bright. "I assume one of you or both of you are responsible for this outrageous prank we've just had to deal with. I will need to have serious words with both of you first thing this afternoon. I'm only thankful that all of the students have been returned to ground level and all in one piece," says Bright forcefully, just before noticing Arthur Crook storm out of the school and approach them all, looking very, very irate.

The headmaster rolls his eyes around with frustration at the approaching Crook. He even quickly considers ways of escaping the school inspector before resigning himself from the idea and realising that he will have to take full responsibility for the events that have just taken place.

Crook arrives. He looks to the two bruised teachers, Heckton and Wade, in front of him, then looks to the headmaster himself.

"I've never seen the like of it! I trust that the fire service has returned all of your pupils to you in one piece?" asks Crook, not waiting for the answer. "I can assure you all that you will never see the likes of this again at this school, for I will recommend that the school be closed by the end of the week. Do you hear me?" adds Crook, looking the headmaster sternly in the eye.

"You're new here, Arthur. You do not fully understand what goes on at this school," replies Geoff, feeling defeated.

"You mean to say that there is more that goes on at this school than all of this that I have just witnessed? Is this a normal Tuesday morning at your school, headmaster? My superiors will never stand for this kind of behaviour ever again," adds Crook, foaming at the mouth.

Headmaster Bright cannot help but rage inside himself at this annoying little school inspector, even though he shows no signs of it. It even takes the intuitive Heckton a while to realise that his former commanding officer in the desert may well be about to blow his top at any minute.

Heckton has seen Bright blow his top only once before but when he did, that was enough to send shivers down Heckton's spine for days. If the headmaster is just about to blow his top once more, then it makes Heckton clearly aware that they could all be in some kind of danger, right here in the middle of the playground, from the headmaster himself, unless the Bright can be placated in some way.

Heckton is therefore more than eager to keep this little man, Crook, quiet as soon as he can, before Anthony Bright unleashes some kind of aggressive act that could shut them all up for good. However, even Heckton cannot stop Crook remaining on the offensive for the time being.

"How can you possibly survive this, headmaster? Students jumping around the school and then jumping into trees and onto roofs, for goodness' sake?" says Crook, unaware of how close the headmaster is to losing his temper.

"Why don't you mind your own business, Crook, you little pipsqueak: you are the one least welcome around here. Why don't you leave us all alone and go back to your dungeon, or wherever it is you inspectors live, and get out of this school for good!" says Geoff, instantly relieving the headmaster of the need for the outburst that was welling up inside him that could well have endangered them all.

Geoff pushes Crook away, causing the little and quite frail man to fall to the ground. Crook gets quickly back to his feet and Geoff is about to push him back down to the ground, when Roger wades in as incensed as the rest of them by Crook's interfering.

"Leave him, Geoff. He's not worth it. He's all mouth," says Roger, half aware that Geoff's acts could well have saved them all from a very angry outburst from the headmaster that could have become very serious indeed. Yet Crook remains defiant but also unaware of how tense things have become out there in the middle of the playground.

"We'll see about that!" says Crook, finally feeling a bit frightened by the four teachers circling around him and standing above him. This feeling eventually makes Crook take a few steps backwards to get away from them all. He can sense that the four of them are turning against him.

"I will report every single thing that has happened at this school since I have been teaching here and I hope to see you all go to jail, let alone out of a job," says

Crook bravely, as he retreats away from them and back towards the school, all the while feeling more and more frightened by the looks Anthony Bright and the other three teachers give him as he retreats.

Crook says no more to them and soon turns away to make his way hastily back towards the school, but as he turns Heckton approaches him and gets in his way. There is a tussle but Crook remains standing, so he runs back towards the school, now feeling quite panicked and gripped by fear. He feels genuinely frightened by the four teachers he has just confronted and wishes, in some ways, that he had not said all of those threatening things that he has just said to them.

By the time he reaches the door to the school, he feels quite certain that he does not want to meet with these teachers ever again, so he pulls open the door then hastily disappears inside, without once looking back at the four teachers he has just threatened with dismissal.

Crook feels a panic take hold of him as soon as he walks through the corridor inside the school. He begins to sweat and he becomes confused by his surroundings. All he wants to do now is to get out of the school and never return to the place.

When he sees other students and teachers approach him in the corridor, he's not even sure where he is any more or what he is doing, so he pushes past the students and the teachers alike as the panic grips him even more strongly.

Crook sees some stairs ahead of him. It looks quieter up at the top of them, so he dashes up the stairs to get away from them all. He climbs and climbs the stairs until he has reached the very top. Then he dashes along the corridor towards the last room at the end to get as far away from them all as he can.

He opens the door to the last room on the top floor to find a small and unused office on the other side. He jumps inside the room then slams the door closed.

He breathes heavily but his panic only seems to be getting worse. He leans against the back of the door pondering over what he has just done, until the panic that he has created for himself fills his body completely.

Crook scrabbles around in his pocket to try and find his mobile phone and call for help but he cannot find it. He panics some more. Then he remembers the tussle in the playground with Heckton. Did Heckton steal his mobile phone?

There's a connected land line phone ahead of him on a table. He puts it to his ear to make sure it works. He looks out of the window yet freezes, because right outside it Max Heckton stands on a ladder, cutting the telephone wire leading out from the office that Crook stands in. The telephone that Crook is holding to his ear immediately goes dead.

Crook then watches Heckton give him one more of his evil, toothy grins while he holds up Crook's mobile phone in his other hand. Heckton did steal his phone! They are all against him, thinks Crook to himself. He slams the landline phone down in a panic, sure that he's upset all of the teachers at this school now and he regrets it all. Why did he not refrain from tackling them head on?

It's too late now though, he realises to himself. What should he do? Is he trapped up here? Does anyone know where he is? Yes, Heckton does, he has just seen him from outside!

Crook looks around the unused room, piled high with books, at the end of the top corridor. He closes the door first of all. There's a key in the lock so he locks it, as well.

He looks outside through the window again. It is too high for him to jump to the ground. Then he hears footsteps outside in the corridor. Heavy, purposeful footsteps that can belong to only one man, the headmaster. Crook freezes. He cannot even move, such is his fear. Oh, why was he so direct with them all in the playground? Why didn't he keep his temper under control?

The heavy footsteps get louder until he can hear them right outside the door to his locked room. Crook holds the key that locked the door in his hand. He soon hears another key outside in the lock. Bright unlocks the door from the other side. The handle to the door slowly lowers and the door slowly opens.

Crook falls over a table as he tries to move to the back of the room to escape. Bright strides into the room with his long black gown billowing around his ankles and traps Crook on the table. He leans over the terrified-looking Crook while the little man cowers beneath him.

"No! No! No!" cries Crook, not knowing what the angry headmaster will do next. The door to the room quickly slams shut on them both and all that can now be heard from inside the room are heavy thuds and scuffles.

Moments later and back inside the room, Anthony Bright locks the cupboard door at the far end of the room, near to the window. There's a *thump, thump, thump* from the inside of the locked cupboard door when Bright walks out of the room and locks its door behind him. He then calmly strides back along the top-floor corridor towards the stairs, leaving the muffled thuds from the inside of the small room at the end of the corridor to fade into nothing.

Chapter 17

Roger enters a sunny staffroom a few weeks later with his face looking much better than it did several weeks before. Even the reddening of his face has faded a little and Roger feels, for some unknown reason, in a good mood when he takes a seat in the staffroom.

Opposite him sits Susan Chalmers. She talks with the very sullen-looking and uncommunicative Mitchell Philpott next to her but unlike most of the other teachers in the room, she easily manages a few hearty laughs after some of the things that Philpott says to her. Her laughs also raise a smile on Mitchell Philpott's face for perhaps the first time this term, when she begins to admire his recently polished, social-mobility scooter.

It is not long before the staffroom door flies open and Max Heckton strides in to give a toothy grin to anyone daring look at him. His face sores have also faded from their reddened glow, just like Roger's, but there is still one sore full of pus that stands out on his chin.

He takes a seat next to Susan Chalmers and huffs into Philpott's face, feeling quite jealous that she gives Philpott so much of her attention. The huff causes the final pus-filled sore on Heckton's face to burst open and make the pus fly out of the sore across the staffroom. Susan follows the flying pus with a disgusted look on her face.

Geoff soon appears in the staffroom doorway looking flustered, confused and as late as always. He walks towards Rose at the far end of the staffroom, not acknowledging any of the other teachers because of his lateness, so he misses Heckton sticking out a leg when he walks past him. Geoff trips over the leg, causing him to fall to the floor.

Geoff picks himself up from the floor, instantly knowing who the culprit is – for who else would it be – but walks on by, ignoring Heckton as best he can, while Heckton hisses like a snake after him.

"What's happened to Crook? They say he's gone. Left under a cloud," says Geoff, feeling panicked when he takes a seat next to Rose.

"I haven't heard anything about Crook, Geoff, and I wouldn't push the headmaster on the matter. He looks in a pretty foul mood, even for him, when I saw him earlier," replies Rose, just as the door to the staffroom swings open and Bright strides in with his long, black gown billowing around his ankles.

Geoff can instantly tell that Rose is right about Bright. He does, indeed, look to be in a foul but also a determined mood and Geoff knows that, for now, he should leave the headmaster well alone.

Then to Geoff's and everyone else's amazement, Arthur Crook walks sheepishly into the staffroom and takes a seat near to the door. Rose's mouth drops open and all the other teachers go quiet.

"I thought we had seen the last of him," says Rose to Geoff quietly.

"So had I," replies Geoff, feeling more panicked than ever. "What do you think it means? He hasn't been seen for weeks and now he turns up like this, as if nothing had ever happened," adds Geoff.

"From what I have heard, the headmaster had a long meeting with him last week," replies Roger, from a seat nearby.

"Why on earth did the headmaster want him back here? He's bound to cause only more problems," says Rose, immediately looking to Geoff, who holds his head in his hands in despair.

Headmaster Bright walks over to his lectern, then once all of the teachers have taken their seats, he addresses his congregation with a forced smile on his face.

"It is the final week before the exams begin so I am looking forward to discovering exactly how hard and well you have all been working during the year. Good luck to you all. Now, there was some commotion amongst certain staff members several weeks ago, which I know has been the only topic of conversation amongst you other teachers, ever since, but I can now assure you that I have spoken with all the staff members concerned and thankfully, we have all reached an agreement to resolve these matters fully, nearer to the end of the school term, so as not to disrupt the exams," says Bright, leaving Geoff to shrug his shoulders as if to say the headmaster hasn't spoken to him.

"I trust that you will all familiarise yourselves with the exam timetable as soon as you receive a copy, which should be sometime today. Now, let's all focus on the upcoming exams and put other matters out of our minds for the time being. Oh, and before I forget, and despite what you may have heard, the end-of-year staff party is still going ahead during the last week of term. It will be a chance for all of us hard-working teachers to let our hair down, so I hope to see you all there," adds Bright with a hopeful and forced smile on his face, before gathering up his papers and striding back out of the staffroom.

Geoff looks to Crook, who purposely avoids his gaze, so Geoff looks to Rose again with great concern before getting up from his seat and leaving the staffroom quietly and as calmly as possible with all of the other teachers.

A week later, the Year Eleven pupils sit quietly, row after row, in the school hall ready to start their first maths exam. Roger stands at the front of the hall.

"You may turn over your papers and begin," says Roger to the students.

Geoff sits next to him, his hands shaking with nerves and his sweaty palms making him feel very uncomfortable. He looks lovingly towards Rose, standing at the back of the hall, but he's still unable to control his nerves while the students bow their heads in front of him and get on with their exam paper.

Geoff is pleased he managed to supply his honeyed refreshments to his students the week before the exams with no problems from Heckton but he looks nervously towards Rose because he did manage to persuade her to do likewise. Did he really need to get her involved in their little scheme as much as he has done? He ponders with regret while his hands continue to shake nervously.

At the end of the first day of exams, Geoff and Rose walk out of the school feeling quite exhausted and both looking it. This does not go unnoticed by Roger, who can't believe that Rose and Geoff would go ahead with their little scheme after the events of a few weeks ago.

What's more, he can't believe that Rose has got more involved, too, despite what he has said and done for her. He just can't believe they would go ahead with their plans and he is absolutely convinced that they have gone ahead with them but for the first time since he has been at the school, he feels he can't inform the headmaster about Geoff because he just couldn't handle the strain of it all any more.

Geoff walks towards his car. "I took a quick peek at a few of their completed maths papers, Rose, and they all looked good to me," he says.

"You looked very nervous before the exam began," replies Rose. "Roger noticed, you know," she adds.

"I'm sure he did," says Geoff.

"We must just keep to the plan, Geoff. They all still have several more exams to do this week but if they complete them successfully, we could both be in for big promotions by the end of term, just like you said we would be," replies Rose, remaining much calmer about the whole ordeal than Geoff.

Geoff again regrets involving Rose with his and Appleby's little scheme and he's half aware that Rose has only got more involved just to make sure he will carry his plan through.

"Just make sure you keep Roger away from me as much as you can. Keep him occupied somehow," says Geoff. "I just couldn't handle him going to the headmaster again with his suspicions."

"I'm sure Roger knows, you know, Geoff. He's just not saying anything this time, but you're right, the less you talk to him the better it will be," replies Rose.

"Right you are, Rose: that suits me," says Geoff, giving her a quick hug that she accepts before she skips away towards Roger's revving Porsche parked on the other side of the car park.

Geoff looks lovingly towards Rose as she skips away from him but his attention is soon grabbed by Susan Chalmers standing on the other side of the car park. Susan and Heckton argue intensely and loudly until Heckton turns his bee-stung, pockmarked face away from her and slopes into his jeep. He looks angry to Geoff and Geoff feels he should walk over to help Susan out, especially when she suddenly bursts into tears once Heckton slams his car door shut and drives his car away from her, leaving her standing on her own.

But Geoff is very aware that he should avoid all contact with Heckton, as well as Roger, as much as possible for the time being, if not for ever, so he leaves Susan in tears on the other side of the car park and unhappily unlocks his car door, just as Roger's Porsche approaches him, throbbing deeply.

Geoff looks pleadingly towards Rose in the passenger seat, wanting her to chuck Roger and return to him, which Rose can read all too easily in Geoff's face.

"Rose!" cries Geoff in desperation towards her, causing tears to fill Rose's eyes when she winds down her window of the passenger seat.

"I'm sorry, Geoff, but Roger and I have decided to move our relationship forward," she says, as she tries to stifle a laugh.

Roger then revs his engine even louder to drown out any reply Geoff may try to make, as he drives his gleaming sports car out of the school.

Feeling quite heartbroken, Geoff watches Roger's Porsche drive away. Just to make matters worse, Roger then speeds his throbbing Porsche away along the road more loudly, even though it cannot now be seen from the school.

Geoff slopes into his battered old car, then sits inside it looking sadly towards his steering wheel. He almost feels like crying but instead, he sees something out of the corner of his eye that captures his attention. He looks up to the church on the other side of the road from the school and to his amazement, he finds Russell Appleby standing on top of the church tower, arms crossed, looking down towards him.

Appleby looks stern and he stares at Geoff until Geoff cottons on that Russell is still very angry about his queen bees being stolen and one of them still not returned.

"I've told you, Russell, one of them escaped. I returned the other one as soon as I could but the escaped one could be anywhere by now. This was weeks ago," says Geoff, more to himself, but hoping Appleby can lip read him, somehow.

Sure enough, Appleby does seem to understand what Geoff has just said to him.

"What can I do?" says Geoff, gesturing towards Appleby standing on top of the church tower. No one else seems to be able to see because of the tall trees that surround the church.

Appleby continues to stare at him angrily but Geoff does get some kind of hint that Appleby may be able to help him find the missing bee. Geoff's concerns for the lost bee had long since diminished but now he knows that Appleby will not be placated until he returns the missing bee. He realises that their current plans may well be at risk if he does not locate Appleby's missing bee as soon as he can, so he decides he will pay Appleby a visit later that evening to try and resolve the matter that has come back to haunt him.

The remaining school exams pass off quietly and without incident and Geoff and Rose feel hugely relieved when the final papers are collected from Year Eleven's final exams.

Geoff has been sneaking a peek at some of their completed papers collected over the weeks and he has informed Rose that their little scheme seems to have worked well, very well indeed, even if he remains quite reserved about the success that will now surely be theirs, when the papers are marked and the exam grades given.

There are now only a few weeks until the end of the school year and the sun shines warmly over Geoff as he walks back towards his car after completing the penultimate week of term.

He feels that he has rescued his year quite well and perhaps even turned things around for himself should the exams be as successful, when marked, as they appear to be when he sneaked a peek at them.

As Geoff gets into his car, he remembers that the end-of-term party looms large next week but even this does not deter him, when he drives slowly out of the car park with a smile on his face at the prospect of his possible promotion. He remembers the meeting with Appleby a few weeks ago and he knows that the missing queen bee still remains at large but Appleby did let him know where it could be found. He has just been so busy that he has not had time to do anything but teach and keep a low profile at the school, lest he upset Max Heckton or Roger Little, who could easily throw a spanner in the works and still get him into trouble.

In fact, the more he thinks about it, the more Geoff wonders why Heckton has not said anything more to the headmaster. Perhaps the headmaster has finally come to his senses and told Heckton to keep as low a profile as Geoff seems to have been keeping and it is this reason, Geoff concludes, that must be the right one, as he drives his old car out of the school car park.

He has almost forgotten about Rose for the time being because of his work load and the other matters on his mind and had he known what the cold-shoulder effect was having on Rose, he would have tried it much earlier on, because it is now Rose's turn to look lovingly towards Geoff as he drives out of the car park, while she slopes into Roger's Porsche.

She feels quite angry that Geoff hasn't been paying her much attention recently and it makes her wonder if he has found another woman, so when he completely ignores the revving Porsche to one side of him in the car park and she notices the broad smile across Geoff's face as he drives out of the car park, she really starts to become quite worried.

While Geoff drives away, smiling broadly, along the road just outside the school and Rose fumes with jealousy inside Roger's Porsche, that's just leaving the school car park, inside the school, Anthony Bright ushers Max Heckton sharply into his office then closes the door behind him.

"Take a seat, Max," says Bright.

Heckton can sense trouble ahead. He has been doing as the headmaster has instructed him to do for the past four weeks, which is to keep well out of the way of the other teachers as much as possible and on no account approach the headmaster for any reason, but Heckton instinctively knows that he is still going to be in trouble.

"It has all been too quiet for my liking recently," says Heckton grumpily.

"Has it? Well, you should realise by now that that is the way I like it, especially during exam season," replies Bright. "Now, Max, I'm afraid I have some bad news for you," says Bright, feeling quite upset but knowing that he must do what he must do.

"Chris Bagshott has contacted you and plans to return to the school?" asks Heckton.

"No, no. On that score, Bagshott has never returned to the school after that little incident in the car park that evening, which I shall never talk about again, I can assure you." replies Bright. "Although even then, I seem to remember that we were correcting something that you yourself had set in motion previously, but I can assure you that that is an end to that particular little matter, Max," adds Bright.

"It is your general behaviour during the year and your constant trouble-making attitude that we must address, Max. I thought that you would have understood my intentions after that little incident with Bagshott, as well as with Crook, the school inspector, but you do not seem to have understood my intentions at all and you have continued to target Geoff Wade and even Roger Little with accusations of foul play," says Bright in full flow.

"I know we go back a long way and you have been very helpful to me over the years, which I am thankful for, but it is now time our relationship came to end. That is why I am letting you go, right here and now, because we cannot afford to have your kind of disruptive behaviour at this school any longer," adds Bright, clearly and forcefully.

"You accuse me of disruptive behaviour? What about Geoff Wade? Rose Daniels, Roger Little? I have been doing my best to help you and keep these trouble-making teachers at bay and under control and this is how you repay me?" replies Heckton angrily.

"I'm afraid I don't see it that way. I see you as the trouble-maker and it is you who must go," says Bright firmly.

"Well, what about Arthur Crook? What is he doing back here? I thought you were doing your best to get rid of him." replies Heckton.

"Ah, well – Arthur Crook has had a change of heart, quite literally. He and Susan Chalmers cannot keep their hands off each other, so I have been told, and it has made him see the light. He has become a valued member of the maths department in the few weeks since he has returned to the school. He has seen the error of his ways and as you are aware, Susan Chalmers has always been very popular since she started here. Her ability in bringing Mitchell Philpott back into the fold after so many issues with his social-mobility scooter has been, quite frankly, incredible," says Bright.

"I can't believe you're saying these things, headmaster. We go back a long way. You were my commanding officer," replies Heckton, almost feeling hurt, if he knew how to feel such a way.

"I understand that, Max, and that is why I have kept you on for so long, out of a sense of loyalty, but loyalty can only be pushed so far. I've been noticing this troublesome and quite frankly unpleasant attitude in you for quite a few years now. You're not in the desert now, Max, and I wouldn't have stood for such behaviour there, anyway. I suggest you leave the teaching for at least a few years and try your hand at something else," says Bright, finally glad that he has put into words what he has been feeling for quite some time.

"I still can't quite believe it, Anthony. After all these years," replies Heckton, who now feels hurt like he has never felt hurt before. Heckton goes silent for a minute. "You mean to tell me that Crook never reported that major incident that happened in the playground?" asks Heckton.

"Not one word. He felt that the school could not cope with such revelations," replies Bright.

"But what about Wade and Rose, and Roger, and what about those bees?" asks Heckton finally.

"What bees? What are you talking about, Max? Just to let you know I've taken a look at Year Eleven's exam papers, like I usually do, and Geoff and Rose look like they have improved their students grades like no other teachers have been able to do at this school, ever before. I see promotions for both of them at the end of the school year and healthy pay rises to go with them," says Bright, getting to his feet, feeling he's said enough. "Thank you for those many years of teaching that you have given to this school and I wish you well in your future endeavours," adds Bright.

Bright then sweeps towards the closed door, opens it, smiles, and then hopes Heckton will leave his office without saying anything more.

Heckton still feels a bit dumbstruck. He doesn't know what to say. His firm support for the headmaster over the years has never wavered. He just can't understand the headmaster's attitude. His anger is such that he still can't think of anything to say right now, so he gets up from his seat then slopes miserably out of the room as quickly as he can.

"Thank you for all your help, once again," says Bright, when Heckton leaves the room. Bright then closes the door and breathes out deeply with relief.

Chapter 18

It is the final week of the school year and inside the school hall one evening of this final week, heavy, deep-bass music pumps out from two, large loudspeakers that stand in two corners of the nineties'-themed hall where decorations hang all around and above them.

The end-of-year staff party is in full swing and the dance floor is packed with sweaty, drunk teachers strutting their stuff. They're all dressed in nineties' clothes and several large moustaches are worn by quite a few of the teachers, including the women.

The dancing is very intense and quite frankly freakish at times, but none of the teachers on the dance floor seem to wonder why the dance routines of some of the teachers that they know so well are so different from their normal behaviour during school hours.

Not to be outdone by this freakish teacher-dancing, Roger Little dances on his hands right in the middle of them all, impressing quite a few of the women around him including the very, very popular Susan Chalmers. Even Valerie Coutt, his fierce competitor in the unofficial 'Best English Teacher at the School' league table, claps with glee at Roger's dance routine that Roger has never even practised before, not once.

Thanks to Susan Chalmers, even Mitchell Philpott has put in an appearance at the end of year party, with his wife Marjorie, quite enthralled by the moves Mitchell manages to produce from his gyrating social-mobility scooter.

His dance-moves soon bring several teachers over to him at one side of the dance floor to cheer him on some more. They give him constant applause for his gyrating scooter while one brave teacher lies down next to a small wooden ramp that has been situated in the corner of the room for a stunt Philpott has already planned for.

Mitchell Philpott is about to demonstrate his party piece to the whole gathering and can't wait. He revs up his social-mobility scooter at one side, while all of those on the dance floor turn to him and stop their freakish dancing for a moment, when they can see Mitchell's about ready to start his stunt.

Mitchell revs up his scooter some more and once he's aware that he is now the centre of attention, he speeds his scooter towards the wooden ramp ahead of him, where a teacher lies flat on the floor of the hall on the other side of the ramp.

Mitchell Philpott's social-mobility scooter drives up the ramp in slow motion and then once it reaches the edge of the ramp, it takes flight. The wheels on his scooter drop slightly as it takes to the air in slow motion, flying over the teacher lying close to the ramp on the other side.

As Philpott does so, the teachers on the dance floor ahead of him open their mouths with wonder, when Mitchell's scooter clears the teacher beneath his wheels and then lands back onto the floor on the other side.

Mitchell then skids his social mobility scooter around, once he has completed his death-defying routine and looks to the other teachers for recognition as they began to applaud and shout his name. "Philpott, Philpott," they chant, in honour of their racy woodwork teacher and his flying-scooter stunt.

Mitchell laps up the applause with joy and he smiles a smile that no one has ever seen him make before. Mitchell is, at last, the main man, which he has secretly wanted to be all of his life, yet his yearning has always been thwarted, up until now, by the health issues that have affected him for so long.

The teacher who had been bravely lying down next to the ramp soon jumps to his feet once the stunt has been completed and fist-pumps the air in victory. "Yeah, yeah!" he shouts with excitement, before going over to Philpott to pat him on the back and congratulate him.

Philpott soon begins to gyrate his scooter more funkily than he has ever gyrated his scooter before, which causes his long-suffering wife to almost faint with excitement.

It is not long before the other teachers return to their freakish and intense dancing, making Roger return to dancing on his hands right in amongst them.

Roger finally sees Rose walk into the deep-pumping music hall and wonders where she has been, so he lifts one hand off the floor to wave at her. Rose rolls her eyes and emits a deep sigh that no one else hears because of the deafening pumping music.

Rose approaches Roger with a quiet disgust written all over her face. She wears a very baggy shirt and a thick moustache, as well as a long-haired wig, but she looks far from being in a party mood and when she sees Roger dancing on his hands in front of her, she feels like turning around and walking straight out again. However, Anthony Bright quickly approaches her from the bar to prevent her leaving.

Bright is half-cut and in a good mood. He's obviously enjoying himself. He's dressed head to toe in eighties' clothes with a bright fluorescent T-shirt on that looks far too small for him and hangs over his beer belly. But he has got the fake moustache right, as well as a tightly hair-curled wig that does seem to make him look a bit more nineties and a bit more like the other teachers at the school social gathering.

"It's a nineties'-themed party, Anthony, not eighties!" shouts Rose to Bright reluctantly, but trying to be as sociable as she can while she looks around the room for Geoff.

"Who would have noticed the difference, except you?" shouts Bright, giving Rose the feeling that he may make a pass at her at any minute.

However, Bright senses Rose may be thinking this, so he returns to matters of a more serious nature. "You know, I did take a quick look at Year Eleven's completed exam papers and their answers looked very impressive indeed, for this school, especially in maths and English. What you have achieved this year could well turn out to be nothing short of a miracle. You should know that in maths, and hang on to your hat, even Lucy Shoreditch may have passed her exams!" shouts Bright to an impressed-looking Rose.

In fact, Rose looks back towards him with astonishment but she says nothing else, because the loud and deep bass sounds coming from the two large speakers reverberate through their bodies making conversation very difficult, as well as making the liquid in their drinks glasses shudder.

Bright feels he must let her know the good news now. "You know, you and Geoff will be in for promotions should the results turn out as to be as good as I expect them to be. Expect a good start to the new school year in September, both of you," says Bright, smiling at her with his bloodshot, red and tired eyes.

Rose raises a faint smile but there is something on her mind that she can't seem to deal with. She can see Susan Chalmers get off with Arthur Crook in the corner of the room and she manages to witness Mitchell

Philpott do some astonishing moves on his social-mobility scooter in the other corner of the room, but she can't see Geoff. *Where is Geoff?* she wonders.

"I asked Russell Appleby along this year, knowing how well he knows you and Geoff but he doesn't seem to have turned up," says Bright. "Apparently that's not unusual for him," he adds, making sure Rose understands whose side he has taken in all of this year's goings-on.

She then faintly remembers she had heard that Max Heckton had been made redundant, which would normally have made her feel better about things but her heart is not with them now in the school hall, not even with Roger, who still dances on his hands ahead of her.

"Where is, Geoff?" says Rose finally.

"Yes, I haven't seen him either. He said he would be here," replies Bright, just about making himself heard and leaving Rose to wonder where Geoff might have got to, just as a heavy, deep-bass rap song begins to thump through their bodies.

When Bright hears the rap song his eyes immediately light up. "This is my song, Rose, I've got to go," he shouts.

Rose half expects the headmaster to go and begin dancing freakishly like the other teachers on the dance floor but to her surprise, he dashes over to the disc jockey, takes a mic from him, then jumps up onto the stage to one side and begins to rap loudly through the mic with the beat of the song, while the other teachers look up to him, open-mouthed with wonder and delight.

"I'm a gangsta rap and I'm gonna rap real hard, I'm gonna rap a message that you ain't gonna see in no card..." raps the headmaster to a delighted and surprised group of enraptured teachers on the dance floor.

Rose has only just arrived but she can stand it no more. She starts to feel ill. She can't stand this change of personality in all of the teachers around her any longer and when she looks to the hand-dancing Roger, ahead of her, she can only feel disgust for him.

She wonders where Geoff might be, then she wonders again, and then she remembers Bright talking of Appleby and she puts two and two quickly together, realising Geoff can be in only one other place.

She dashes out of the school hall as quickly as she can, dropping her beer on the floor in the process and with her eyes full of tears. She leaves Roger to fall onto the dance floor behind her and wonder where on earth she is going. Roger gets onto his knees and watches Rose run out of the school hall. He feels insulted by her rejection of him and he quickly appreciates that their relationship could well be at an end.

Under a deep-red sunset on a very warm summer's evening, Geoff gets out of his battered old car, parked on the gravel driveway of Appleby's farmhouse, holding a holdall that contains the deep hum of the erstwhile missing queen bee. He sweats with the strain of catching the elusive bee but he is relieved to have finally found it and captured it.

He wears thick rubber gloves over his nineties' themed clobber as he carries the holdall through the trees towards the bee hives in the distant fields of Appleby's farm.

His long-haired wig keeps falling into his eyes and his moustache itches like crazy but he has no thought of removing them, for he's still hoping to get back to the school party as soon as he's delivered the missing queen bee back to her hive.

The two larger bee hives loom tall and shadowed ahead of Geoff, under the moonlight, as he approaches them. He can hear the deep hum from inside and the fear of these large bees returns to him quickly.

Thanks to a pub meeting with Appleby earlier that day, Appleby told him where he could find the other queen bee because he had seen it with his own eyes, he told Geoff in the pub earlier.

Whether Appleby did see the queen bee with drunken eyes or sober eyes doesn't concern Geoff because Geoff was sure, at the time, that Appleby did see it. That is why his car contained the bee keeper's outfit necessary for the venture ahead of him later that day.

"Why have you not got hold of this queen bee and taken it back yourself?" asked Geoff of Appleby in the Farmer's Chair public house earlier.

However Geoff soon understands why not, because he soon catches on that Appleby has always been far more interested in the glass of beer ahead of him on the bar counter than his successful and innovatory honey-making business.

When Appleby reaches inside his tweed jacket pocket to pull out a thick wad of money to pay for his next round of drinks earlier that day, something else occurs to Geoff that quite astounds him. He has not shared one drop of beer with Appleby since he had been in that particular public house where the meeting they had could well have lasted for more than two hours.

When he ponders over this thought some more, as he walks through the darkness towards the bee hives, it also dawns upon him that he has had very few alcoholic beverages anywhere and with anyone for what could be almost six weeks, give or take a few days.

No wonder Rose has been paying him more attention recently, it dawns upon him, even though he hadn't realised it at the time because he had been too wrapped up in exam season at school. When he does think about it some more though, he remembers it did bring a smile to his face in the pub earlier that day.

"You don't really care about this queen bee, do you? I thought you did?" asked Geoff of the drunken Appleby in the public house earlier.

"My other queen bee and her friends are performing as well as needed, thank you very much, Geoff. I know you need to capture this queen bee more than I do, for it was all your fault in the first place that she escaped, so I have left the job for you to do," replies Appleby. "I certainly don't want to be stung by that mother of an angry bee. I've certainly had enough bee stings to last me a life time," he adds.

Geoff remembers the events in the pub earlier because they somehow make him all the more determined to take this queen bee back to where it belongs and set matters straight with Appleby.

Geoff can now see and hear the large bees hum around the two tall bee hives and it's a good job he feels determined to see the task through, because his fear of these bees is more acute now than ever.

Then he remembers he hasn't put his bee-keeper's protector outfit on. In his haste, he has left it lying on the back seat of his car. He has the rubber gloves on to protect his hands but he has forgotten to put the rest of his protective clothing on, including the head-protector. Geoff ponders whether he should go back and put the clothing on but he knows that if he went back to his car now, he would never have the courage to return to the hives.

He soon finds a small ladder leaning against the tall bee hive which does not contain a queen bee so he stumbles towards it, thinking only of returning the queen bee to her hive as quickly as possible, despite already being stung several times by her friends buzzing around him.

The ladder feels unbalanced as soon as Geoff begins to climb it and he wishes he had done the task in the daylight instead of waiting until the gloom of dusk to fulfil Appleby's wishes.

He still holds the holdall containing the queen bee in one hand but as he slowly climbs the ladder to reach the top of the tall bee hive, he can feel the ladder beneath him give way. The ladder then quickly collapses, sending him and the now-open holdall containing the queen bee, crashing down into the very centre of the mostly empty bee hive.

Geoff cries out with pain and fear when he looks up into the moonlight from the destroyed wooden bee hive that lies beneath him and around him, because bees from both hives soon swarm around him and pepper him with stings.

When the returned queen bee flies out of the holdall next to him, to escape once more, it does not bother him again and instead flies out of the collapsed bee hive and away into the night, leaving Geoff to be stung many, many times more before the other bees take flight and follow their returned queen into the night.

Geoff looks to the bees swarming all around him and despite his fall, his moustache and long-haired wig remain attached, but the developing pain of the stings and the fear they invoke in him eventually cause Geoff to faint, while he still lies in the very centre of the crushed bee hive.

Roger's loud, revving Porsche soon wheelspins onto the gravel driveway of Appleby's farmhouse in hearing distance of the hives. The sports car then skids to a halt as close to the kitchen door of the farmhouse as it can. Rose hastily jumps out of the passenger seat then dashes towards the trees.

Roger jumps out of his car on the other side. "No, Rose, it's too dangerous. I can hear the bees from here!" shouts Roger after her, when she disappears into the darkness.

Rose runs fearlessly and unthinkingly through the fields towards the dangerously humming bee hives, shadowed under the moonlight in the distance. She does not think of the fear she feels: she only thinks of one thing – Geoff, being stung by all of those bees.

She arrives at the tall bee hives to find Geoff lying unconscious on top of the collapsed bee hive. Bees still hover around him but Rose jumps in fearlessly and pulls Geoff's unconscious body away from the bee hive and as far away as she can drag him, not even aware that Roger helps drag Geoff to safety with her.

Once Rose has dragged Geoff far enough away from the bee hive as she can, she kisses him and tries to wake him, but Geoff remains unconscious.

"I've called for an ambulance, Rose," says Roger.

Rose does not seem to hear him as she removes Geoff's moustache and long-haired wig, so as to give him more air to breathe.

"Rose! Can you hear me, Rose?" says Roger, leaning over Geoff to check him over too, but Rose still cannot hear him. All she can think about is Geoff lying out cold in front of her, so she kisses him again, this time deep with worry.

Roger soon hears the sirens of the ambulance in the distance and he knows that he has finally been defeated in trying to win Rose's affections. It has always been in the back of Roger's mind that Geoff might win her back one day, so when he sees them there together in the darkness, he says no more to Rose and leaves her alone with the unconscious Geoff.

He trudges back through the fields and trees towards his precious Porsche, parked in the farmhouse driveway, feeling very low indeed. Roger then opens the door of his Porsche as the blaring sirens and flashing lights of the ambulance skid to a halt on the gravel driveway right next to him.

He puts one leg on the ledge of the car door while resting his arms and hands on its roof. He then puts his shades on, even though it is dark, and looks towards the bright moon above and the swaying trees around him, knowing that he has lost Rose for good, to the one man he always feared would win her back – Geoff Wade.

Behind him, two paramedics jump out of the ambulance then dash towards the trees, thanks to Roger's pointing finger. Roger then slopes into his Porsche and drives slowly out of the driveway, back over the gravel, then back onto the country lane. His sports car does not rev its engine like it usually does; in fact, it remains very quiet indeed, for a sports car, until the rear lights of the Porsche fade away into the night.

The two paramedics arrive very swiftly by Rose's side as they swipe away the stinging bees as bravely as Rose did. They then quickly administer the life-saving drugs to Geoff, slowly bringing him round.

"Oh, Geoff, Geoff! What were you thinking?" says Rose, hugging him, while Geoff still says nothing. "He is going to make it, isn't he?" asks Rose of the paramedics.

"Oh, he'll make it," replies one of the paramedics, helping Geoff onto a stretcher.

"Oh, Geoff, I will never leave you alone again, ever," says Rose, with tears in her eyes that eventually give way to a full cry. "I love you, Geoff. I have always loved you," she declares, while they carry Geoff back through the trees towards the ambulance.

The two paramedics then manhandle Geoff into the ambulance and allow Rose to jump inside the ambulance, too. The paramedic then closes the ambulance door and the ambulance drives swiftly out of the drive and away along the country lane with its flashing blue lights piercing the darkness.

The sun shines brightly over a field full of tall wheat that blows in a gentle breeze the next evening. A skylark takes flight and wrestles with the wind that blows through the large flat field, then over the houses at the edge of the field and then finally over the last house on the corner of that field, where a much calmer and peaceful-looking Max Heckton tends to his herbaceous borders in his well-manicured garden.

The approaching skylark makes Heckton look upwards into the evening sky, making the last of his unhealed pus-filled sores to burst open and release a yellow-coloured pus that drips all over his shirt. This distracts him for a moment.

Heckton then looks again into the sky, but this time he is sure that it is not a skylark that flies towards him, yet he can't quite make out, just yet, what is flying his way.

Heckton focuses on the flying thing above him until finally he gives a teeth-filled grin, for he knows what it is. The deep humming of the oversized queen bee eventually reaches Heckton's ears and for some reason he instinctively opens his mouth.

The large queen bee flies downwards towards him and doesn't think twice about flying straight into his mouth, whereupon Heckton crunches down hard onto it. Heckton chomps onto the large bee with relish. He then crunches some more until his face freezes and his eyes widen with fear as the large queen bee stings him inside his mouth.

The wind blows on through the field of fully grown wheat, under a setting sun, until the skylark can be heard singing in the distance high in the sky somewhere unseen.